FUGITIVE OF TIME

Borgo Press Books by JOHN RUSSELL FEARN

1,000-Year Voyage: A Science Fiction Novel
Anjani the Mighty: A Lost Race Novel (Anjani #2)
Black Maria, M.A.: A Classic Crime Novel
The Crimson Rambler: A Crime Novel
Don't Touch Me: A Crime Novel
Dynasty of the Small: Classic Science Fiction Stories
The Empty Coffins: A Mystery of Horror
The Fourth Door: A Mystery Novel
From Afar: A Science Fiction Mystery
Fugitive of Time: A Classic Science Fiction Novel
The G-Bomb: A Science Fiction Novel
The Gold of Akada: A Jungle Adventure Novel (Anjani #1)
Here and Now: A Science Fiction Novel
Into the Unknown: A Science Fiction Tale
Last Conflict: Classic Science Fiction Stories
Legacy from Sirius: A Classic Science Fiction Novel
The Man from Hell: Classic Science Fiction Stories
The Man Who Was Not: A Crime Novel
One Way Out: A Crime Novel (with Philip Harbottle)
Pattern of Murder: A Classic Crime Novel
Reflected Glory: A Dr. Castle Classic Crime Novel
Robbery Without Violence: Two Science Fiction Crime Stories
Rule of the Brains: Classic Science Fiction Stories
Shattering Glass: A Crime Novel
The Silvered Cage: A Scientific Murder Mystery
Slaves of Ijax: A Science Fiction Novel
Something from Mercury: Classic Science Fiction Stories
The Space Warp: A Science Fiction Novel
The Time Trap: A Science Fiction Novel
Vision Sinister: A Scientific Detective Thriller
What Happened to Hammond? A Scientific Mystery
Within That Room!: A Classic Crime Novel

FUGITIVE OF TIME

A CLASSIC SCIENCE FICTION NOVEL

JOHN RUSSELL FEARN

THE BORGO PRESS
MMXII

FUGITIVE OF TIME

FIRST BORGO PRESS EDITION

Published by Wildside Press LLC

www.wildsidebooks.com

DEDICATION

To the memory of Ian Dick

CONTENTS

INTRODUCTION

by PHILIP HARBOTTLE

After John Russell Fearn's instant success with *Operation Venus*, his first science fiction novel to be published by the London firm of Scion Ltd. in May 1950, Scion's Managing Director travelled to Fearn's Blackpool home, and talked him into signing a five-year contract to write more science fiction novels—exclusively for Scion, under the contractual pen name of 'Vargo Statten'. The only exception was that Fearn was allowed to continue to write for his lucrative main overseas market, the Toronto *Star Weekly*. Since their novels were published as a tabloid newspaper weekly insert in the *Star Weekly* magazine, they were not one of Scion's paperback competitors.

So Fearn continued to appear from Scion as 'Vargo Statten' with increasing regularity: eight sf titles in 1950, ten in 1951, and fourteen in 1952. In the Autumn of 1952 there was a sudden hiatus: Scion were fined for obscenity in one of their gangster titles, and the directors argued about who should pay the fine, eventually falling out and splitting into three splinter groups. For a time Scion were financially very rocky indeed, and looked like going under. Author payments were suspended, and Fearn found himself owed for six novels, to the tune of over 300 pounds (a considerable sum in those days, which would have been worth over 10,000 pounds today). He promptly terminated his contract, as he was entitled to do, and called in the Society of Authors to collect his debt.

The founder of Scion Ltd., B. Z. Immanuel, retained his company offices in London at Kensington High Street, but lost control of the company. He formed his own imprint, Gannet Press. Scion passed to Director Lou Benjamin, who continued the company out of their warehouse at Avonmore Road. Ex-Scion editor Maurice Read headed a consortium of disaffected Scion authors, and formed a third enterprise, Milestone Publications.

Fearn's success was well known among other publishers, and once it became known that he was free of his binding contract to Scion, he was inundated with sf commissions. He was asked to write novels for Curtis Warren, Hamilton & Co. (Panther Books), Pearson's, and Milestone Publications (who planned to have Fearn continue writing as Vargo Statten for them). Read had been quickly off the mark, seeking to poach Scion's two star sf authors, Fearn and E. C. Tubb (who had been writing for Scion as Volsted Gridban). Milestone also secured Scion artist Ron Turner for their sf cover artwork.

Fearn had recently sold a science fiction novel, *Deadline*, to the Toronto *Star Weekly*, and decided that it would be ideal for his first Vargo Statten novel for Milestone. But before the novel would be suitable for Milestone, it needed to be considerably abridged. Fearn did this himself, by retyping the novel to a shorter length. He also gave it a new title for its first book edition—*Fugitive of Time*.

Fearn had accepted all of the commissions he had been offered, and quickly wrote two novels for both Curtis Warren and Pearson's. For Hamilton's he wrote what was intended as the first of a new series (under his own name), featuring a futuristic 'fixer' named Simon Oscar Slade, but by the time the first novel (*Moons for Sale*) had been written, Scion Ltd. had new financial backers who were determined to reclaim their best authors.

Fearn was quickly paid the outstanding sum he was owed, and was offered pay *in advance* for his future work (two sf books a month), which was unheard of in those times. His contract (only two of the five years stipulated had passed) was rewritten to allow Fearn more freedom with his writing (his exclusivity to Scion was to be limited to science fiction, leaving him free to write in other genres for other publishers). But a condition of the new deal was that Fearn had to withdraw his Milestone and Hamilton novels and pass them on to Scion. In retrospect, Fearn might have been better off freelancing, but given the publishing climate at the time, he could scarcely be blamed for 'selling out.'

Scion then set about stopping Milestone from using the 'Vargo Statten' and 'Volsted Gridban' bylines as house names—and succeeded, but only after two 'Gridban' novels by E. C. Tubb had slipped through, *Planetoid Disposals Ltd.*, and *Fugitive of Time*. This latter was *not* the Fearn story (which later appeared from Scion in May 1953 as *Zero Hour* by 'Statten'). Milestone had already purchased a hand-lettered illustrative cover by Ron Turner, so they asked Tubb to write another novel on which they could use the cover (and to complete the complex tale, Ron Turner also later did the cover artwork for *Zero Hour* as well—same scene, but different cover!).

Scion gave Fearn the now-exclusive 'Gridban' byline as well, the idea being that he would be writing full-time under his two names for Scion, and would be unable to capitalize on his new contract clause to write non-science fiction for other companies. Thus *Moons for Sale* became his first 'Gridban' novel in May of 1953.

Meantime, *Deadline* had been published in the *Star Weekly* for December 13, 1952. It is undoubtedly one of Fearn's best stories, working brilliantly as both a science fiction story and as a mystery/suspense novel. Gordon Fryer is a man who discovers the exact future moment when he is due to die at a relatively young age, and sets out to change his own history. The scientific process that reveals his demise also provides photographs of him at future intervals. Despite Fryer's best efforts, each of the photographs becomes a true record, and suspense builds as the deadline of the final photograph comes ever nearer....

The 1953 Vargo Statten version of the story was translated, first in France in 1955, and then the following year in Italy by Patrizio Dalloro (from the French). Interestingly, the Italian publisher, Mondadori, did not issue it as a science fiction novel, but put it out in their modern novel lists. In the 1970s and 1980s the novel was also republished in France by Aredit *as a graphic novel* (as were many other of his Scion novels translated in the French *Anticipation* series of novels). So highly did the comic strip publishers regard the story, that instead of abridging it to fit a single volume, they split it into two episodes, and published it, unabridged, in two separate volumes. A few years later it was reissued in a single double-sized volume. The quality of the novel was further attested when I sold it to F. A. Thorpe in England, who published it in their Linford Mystery Library series in 2006.

When I retyped the novel for submission to Thorpe, I noticed for the first time that there were considerable differences in the text between the *Star Weekly* and Scion paperback versions. A careful study of them (together with Fearn's original correspondence) revealed something very interesting! Fearn had originally written the novel to a length in excess of 45,000 words, which the *Star Weekly* had skilfully condensed to 40,000 words. But in the meantime Fearn himself had rewritten and condensed the novel even further (to only 36,000 words) for its UK book publication. Here and there Fearn had deleted different passages, so that *each version contained text that was missing from the other*! In my own retyping from the longer *Star* version, I carefully restored any additional text that was in *Zero Hour*. The final mss. came out at almost 44,000 words, almost completely restored to its original form, and consequently read even better than any previously published version.

I have always considered it a pity that this novel was fated never to be published with its original Ron Turner cover and former title, *Fugitive of Time*. Some years ago, I even commissioned Ron Turner to recreate his cover painting, for just this purpose. But it is only now, with Borgo Press publishing many of the best of Fearn's novels in the U.S.A. for the first time, that the opportunity has at last arisen!

I am proud to present to new readers one of Fearn's best novels under its original title and with its original cover painting!

—Philip Harbottle,
Wallsend, England,
2012

CHAPTER ONE

THE PHOTOGRAPHS

The advertisement was not very attractively worded since it commenced with the words 'Guinea Pig wanted'. But when at length Gordon Fryer read it all, his interest stirred slightly:

> *Guinea Pig wanted. Male. Between 20 and 30. Must be intelligent. Scientific experiment. Positively no danger. Monetary Reward. Apply: Dr. Boden Royd, The Larches, Nether Bolling, Berks.*

It was a spring morning in 2006 when Gordon Fryer read the advertisement, and the more he thought about it the more it seemed to fit in with his need—which was certainly desperate. A long run of bad luck had practically made him penniless, the London engineering firm for which he worked had gone into liquidation, and Gordon Fryer was flat broke. Hence St. James Park this sunny morning, a daily paper lifted from the nearby wastebasket, and now this.

Gordon Fryer did not look like a guinea pig. He was quite good-looking, black-haired, blue-eyed, ruddy-cheeked.

"Nether Bolling, Berkshire," he mused. "Fair distance from London. Might thumb a ride and see if there's anything in this."

So he got up from the park bench, and thwacking the paper against his thigh, marched vigorously to the main thoroughfare. In another hour, his walk less vigorous, he had gained the city environs and began to look about him for a vehicle. He found it at length when, using up his last reserves, he had lunch at a motel. The burly driver consuming hash next to him would be passing through Nether Bolling on his way to Reading.

"Know anything about a Doctor Royd?" Gordon asked.

"Can't say I do, chum. What is 'e? Medical bloke?"

"He lives at the Larches in Nether Bolling. There my information ends."

The driver shrugged. "Nether Bolling's a cockeyed sort of dump. 'Bout four cottages, a few big swank houses, and that's it. Sort of place you'd find 'ermits."

"I see. Good of you to give me a lift."

"Think nothin' of it. You don't get far in this world—or the next—if you don't 'elp folks out now an' again."

So Gordon Fryer received his lift, seated in the cab of the truck as it sped through the green lanes where the buds were ripening with the promise of summer. It was toward two o'clock when Gordon alighted in Nether Bolling and took his farewell of the lorry driver.... And the driver had been right. Nether Bolling was definitely nothing more than a scattering of cottages, farms, and—quite isolated—tall and dignified residences set well back behind still bare-looking trees.

Not knowing a larch from an elm, and certainly not guided by the leaves at this time of year, Gordon had to inspect each solemn-looking residence before he discovered the right one.

It was a mansion of an early period, well kept, the grounds laid out by experts. Gordon walked up the long drive and pressed the gleaming brass of the bell button at the front door.

He waited, and at length, the polished oak portal opened silently, and a tall, hatchet-faced being with somewhat distended nostrils looked out into the sunlight.

"Your pleasure, sir?" he enquired.

"I'm Gordon Fryer. Dr. Royd is asking for a guinea pig."

"A—" Understanding dawned on the butler's cadaverous face as he saw the newspaper Gordon was carrying. "Oh, yes, sir. Will you kindly step inside?"

Gordon obeyed, stepping into an enormous hall overweighed with massive furniture, armor, and costly antiques. He found himself wondering, whilst he waited, what kind of a profession Dr. Royd could be in to boast all these evidences of wealth. Then the butler returned.

"If you will step this way, sir?"

Gordon did so and presently entered a magnificent library. The door closed quietly. Gordon's preconceived notion of some fiftyish man with a prosperous waist-line and large cigar was instantly destroyed. Instead, he beheld a quiet-looking man of apparent middle age, his gray hair untidy, his suit creased, his pale gray eyes peering over the tops of old-fashioned steel-rimmed spectacles. He had been seated working at his desk, but he rose to his feet with extended hand as Gordon entered.

"Good afternoon, Mr. Fryer! Have a seat— That's it!"

Gordon obeyed. Somehow he could not imagine himself doing anything else but as he was told while dealing with this amiable-looking old codger with the high-pitched, meandering voice.

"So you wish to be a guinea-pig, do you?" Dr. Royd reseated himself at the desk.

"I don't want to be, sir. I have no choice."

"What prompted you to answer my advertisement?"

"I answered it for the simple reason that I have no money. I'm out of a job and they're hard to come by at the moment in my profession—"

"What is your profession?"

"I have none right now. Normally I'm a mechanical engineer. They're ten-a-penny at the moment, as you know."

"No, I don't know. I don't know anything, really, unless it directly relates to my interests. I'm a scientist, Mr. Fryer, as you will have gathered from my adver-tisement. I am a doctor of physics, not medicine. If anything is wrong with you physically, I wouldn't be able to diagnose it."

Gordon smiled uncomfortably. "I—I wouldn't expect you to, Dr. Royd. But in regard to the advertisement, I'm quite willing."

Royd peered over his spectacles. "Are you? To do what?"

"Whatever you want, sir. You said a scientific experiment. You want somebody intelligent. I hope I am reasonably that."

"Yes, yes, I'm sure you are. Forgive my vagueness, young man, but I haven't spoken to anybody for months, outside the servants. Been utterly absorbed. You get that way viewing the future."

"Yes, I suppose you—" Gordon stared. "Doing what?"

Dr. Royd chuckled in high falsetto. "My apologies. Maybe I shouldn't have sprung it on you like that! However, physically and mentally I think you will meet my requirements. What age are you?"

"Twenty-five."

"Quite satisfactory. Ever had a serious illness?"

"Never. I'm fit, intelligent, and willing. My only trouble is lack of money."

"And if you had money you wouldn't be here?" Royd questioned. "Is that it? You are not just here because a scientific experiment appeals to you?"

"In a way it does appeal to me, yes. As an engineer it is bound to. I—er—look, sir, what do I have to do?"

"Well now, I'll explain." Royd sat back in his chair. "I am a scientific inventor, with all the money I need to follow that inclination. Unearned money by inheritance from my dear father, who considered science the invention of the devil. No matter. To put it briefly, I have found a way to view future time, but I cannot be sure whether it applies just to my own state of consciousness or whether it can be universal. I have nobody who is willing to help me out. Not even Blessington, my indispensable manservant, who is privately of the opinion that I am cracked."

"Which makes two of us," Gordon murmured to himself, endeavoring to look interested.

"Time," Royd continued absently, hitching himself forward and jamming a bony knee against the desk edge, "is not something to be experienced as we progress: it is something into which we grow in the natural course of unending evolution."

"Indeed?" Gordon asked, feeling he should say something.

Royd looked over his spectacles. "You haven't the vaguest idea what I'm talking about, have you? I'll try it another way."

Gordon only nodded this time, trying to decide which head needed examining—his or Dr. Royd's.

"Actually," Royd said, "Time is not something which unfolds. The past, present, and future are here this very moment. But with every second our brains are shedding tissue that makes us capable of seeing what we think is advancing Time. In reality it has always been there: we are only just seeing it! The process is allied to the decay that brings senility, but we will not go into that now. After all, our bodies shed something every second that we live—hair, water, surface skin. So why shouldn't the brain?"

For Gordon something dim stirred on the face of the deep and he made a grab at it.

"You mean, sir, that our brains actually have everything stored up in them—future time as well as present—and that this shedding business merely reveals more? Or rather makes us conscious of something which we believe has only just happened?"

Dr. Royd beamed. "My boy, you and I will get along fine! You have a ready grasp of the position. Yes, that is it exactly. By tomorrow our brains will have lost more of their covering and therefore more will be apparent to us—but we will say that Time has moved on. Which is quite erroneous. And, of course, the more shedding there is, the remoter becomes an earlier impression, hence memory fades with advancement."

Gordon's brows knitted. "How far does one see the future?"

"Only as far as one's lifetime. That is obvious. The brain cannot contain impressions of a Time when the brain action itself is extinct."

"In which case one might know when one is going to die?"

"Yes. I know exactly when I shall die—and how and where. In my laboratory, seven in the evening, at the age of ninety-three on the sixteenth of May."

Gordon smiled weakly. "You're very cheerful about it!"

"Why not? To know when you are going to die eliminates all fear of immediate decease. I have about thirty-three years left yet, so I can afford to be cheerful."

"Then—then what exactly do you wish me to do?"

"I wish to see if it is possible to briefly strip your brain as I have my own, in order to view the future scenes of your life. The scenes are there, you understand, and only need uncovering. The process is painless and electrical. I know I can do it on myself, but as I say, I cannot lay this invention before the Institute of Scientists until I know it can be applied to anybody who desires it. If it is peculiar to me alone, then—" Royd spread his hands.

"And there's no danger?" Gordon asked uneasily.

"You have my assurance on that. So much so I shall not even ask you to sign a document absolving me from blame if anything should happen to you. Nothing can. It is merely Nature's process speeded up."

"I—see." Gordon could not keep the doubt out of his voice, at which Dr. Royd got to his feet.

"Come with me, Mr. Fryer. I'll show you what I mean."

Gordon followed the scientist as he toddled from the library, muttering unintelligible comments as he went. Leading the way across the great hall, he finally paused at a door and opened it. Beyond was a big laboratory, brilliantly sun-lit through high skylights. There was a vast array of gleaming equipment, but to Gordon, though he was an engineer, most of it was alien to him.

"Now," Royd said, pausing at an object exactly like

a gigantic enlarging camera poised over a screwed-down chair. "This is the Brain-Scanner, as I call it. When you are seated in the chair, the vibrations peculiar to that instrument are directed downwards into the brain, and according to the wavelength of the vibration used, higher or lower portions of the accumulated layer of brain-cells are penetrated. I have said that in the normal process they shed themselves, which is true. In this instance they are not shed, because that would create permanent injury and make you only capable of seeing the particular period that had been exposed. So, then, the vibration strikes through the top cell layers and photographs whatever image is in the cells below."

"Photographs?" Gordon repeated, astonished.

"Just so. You don't marvel at an X-ray photographing the inside of a body without harming the outside, do you? Why marvel at this striking through the upper layers of cells to photograph the scenes beneath?"

"The marvel to me, sir, is that anything can photograph what must really be only abstract! Surely you can't get a picture of a future scene, or any scene at all, by just photographing a bunch of brain cells?"

"No, of course not." Dr. Royd looked contrite. "Forgive me, young man, but I get in the habit of accepting things and not explaining the parts between. The point is: brain cells give forth vibrations which, when interpreted by the nervous system, form into pictures, sensations, sight, hearing, and so on. Correct?"

"I can gather that much, yes."

"Then there is still hope. Very well; if you have an

instrument which duplicates the system used by the human body for interpreting brain sensations, what do you get?"

"A similar effect as a body would, I suppose."

"Exactly. And here is the main instrument."

Royd moved across to a rotund tower of complicated apparatus.

To Gordon's wondering eyes it even looked vaguely human in outline.

Royd said: "Duplicating the functions of a human body mechanically is one of the simplest things to science. I have done that and added inventions of my own. Summing up, when my vibrations penetrate the brain, it takes a reading of the cells being examined and their vibrations are transmitted to this machine. They interpret the vibrations as the body would, and produce the same result. But instead of a picture forming mentally, it is finally produced visibly by specially designed transformers, so that what an eye would normally see is instead photographed, camera-wise."

"And you get a sort of snapshot of the scene 'penetrated'?"

"Yes. For example—"

Dr. Royd moved to a filing cabinet, shuffled a series of manilla folders for a while, and then returned with half-a-dozen matte-surfaced prints in full plate size. Gordon took them, studied them, and still wondered what he ought to think. They showed Royd in various postures, in various surroundings, but there was certainly nothing to suggest but what the photographs could have been taken in the ordinary way. They were remarkably clear too, very much like the 'stills' put out by a film studio.

"You think I'm crazy, don't you? That these photographs are so many red herrings?" Royd gave a dry smile. "I can assure you that they are perfectly genuine and have been photographed directly from my own brain. I appear each time because I cannot escape holding my body in my thoughts. Nobody can. We would vanish if we didn't."

"Uh-huh," Gordon agreed, and handed the prints back.

"These photos," Royd added, "illustrate scenes from my future life where, at one time or another, I shall find myself doing exactly as the scenes depict. I don't expect you to believe me, but you can prove it by letting me take a scene from your future life. If it works, then anybody on this planet can see a scene from their future life if they wish."

There was a long silence, and it persisted even after Royd had put the photographs back in their folders. Gordon paced about the laboratory, studying the apparatus, all the time watched by the scientist's half-amused gray eyes.

"What is the pay for this experiment?" Gordon asked finally.

"How much did you anticipate? Name your figure."

"That's difficult: but for nerve strain, expenses, and being unable to rid myself of the fear of death, I'd say it's worth five thousand pounds."

"I'll make it ten, payable now to show you I keep faith."

Gordon opened his mouth and then closed it again. By the time he had finished another circuit of the laboratory, he found the check was being thrust into his hand.

"Thanks," he said, nodding. "Now, do I strip or anything?"

"Gracious, no! Just sit in that chair. I don't even have to darken the room."

Gordon sat down slowly and found the chair no more uncomfortable than that of a hairdresser's. There was, however, a certain anguish as he waited whilst Royd fussed about with his apparatus.

"Twenty-five, you say? Right: that means an expectation of life of say fifty years. We'll have a look at fifty years hence and see what there is."

Generators hummed, switches sizzled and snapped, then Gordon found himself in a brief golden glare which dazzled him. His scalp crawled as though mites were creeping in his hair.

"Fortunately," Royd said, switching off again, "I have devised an instantaneous developing and printing system so there will be no waiting."

Gordon glanced. "There's no more to it than this?"

"No more. I told you it was perfectly safe."

Gordon sat back happily. Ten thousand pounds in his pocket and a glorified sun-ray treatment. Money for jam!

"Mmmm," said Royd presently. "You'll evidently be dead at seventy-five."

Gordon sat up again with a jerk. "Eh?"

The scientist came over with a damp print in his fingers. It was totally black.

"This means your brain doesn't register at the age of seventy-five," he explained, "which inevitably means it's got no impressions. At seventy-five you will be dead."

Gordon shrugged. "Oh, well, that's fifty years off, so I'm not bothered. Try something else."

"Yes.... Let me see— We'll try sixty-five."

Again the golden glow, the fast developing process, and a totally black print.

"Sorry," Royd sighed. "You'll be dead at sixty-five, too."

"This," Gordon said uneasily, "is getting a bit too much for me! Sure the thing's working?"

"Definitely! We'll try ten years earlier."

They did. But fifty-five and forty-five were both blank. By this time Gordon was perspiring freely.

"Are you sure I'm alive at all?" he demanded.

"Eh?" Royd peered over his spectacles. "Oh, yes. You're alive but you won't be twenty years hence. Sorry, young man, but this machine is quite ruthless. Maybe we've done enough."

"Enough! I haven't done anything yet! I've sat here and been fried, and all I've seen has been these damned black prints. Try—try something else."

"I could try tomorrow," Royd said, hesitating.

"Okay. If that's a blank as well, it must mean I'm going to commit suicide—or else the thing only works on your brain and not mine."

"That is what I must find out. All right, here we go."

The process was so familiar to Gordon by now that he did not even blink—but he did when he saw the photograph that was handed to him. It depicted him in a white smock busy at a bench in the very laboratory where he now sat.

"Yes, it's me!" He gave a whistle of amazement. "This is uncanny! Anyway, what would I be doing here tomorrow? I'll be back in London."

Royd shook his head. "You'll be here if this says so. You cannot change the law of constant-Time."

"I—I see. I suppose you can't, really."

"Young man, would you allow me to probe further? I wish to be sure where your continuity ends. In other words, I would like to know when you are going to die. If you do not wish to know the date or time, I will withhold them from you. The picture will not tell you that. But for my own satisfaction, I wish to be sure that those earlier photographs were the outcome of genuine obliteration and not due to a technical fault."

"All right, Doc, it's your money. And don't give me the answer."

Royd switched on, this time using a different type of lens in the apparatus, presumably to find the exact 'end of continuity' he wanted without a lot of probing. At the end of five minutes, he switched off again and stood waiting for the print to be ejected. When it came he studied it and frowned.

Gordon got slowly out of the chair and came over to see the photograph for himself. He started when he did so. It showed the interior of a railway compartment, apparently first class, with two windows visible and flaring light outside. On one window in reverse was a label saying YBGUR, which Gordon quickly turned around in his mind to read RUGBY.

He himself—for he recognized his own features, even though they were plumper and very prosperous-looking—was half slumped from the seat of the compartment, his left arm dangling. On the wrist was a curiously fashioned gleaming watch pointing to 11:03. He was attired in a check overcoat, which had fallen away to reveal a dress suit and bow tie beneath.

"I'll be damned!" he exclaimed blankly. "That my death scene?"

"Yes," Royd agreed quietly.

"So I'll pass out on a train going to Rugby, shall I?"

"At eleven-three, according to that watch. Post meridian, to judge from the darkness outside the window. From the bright light from the carriage, I'd say it might be a train smash with flames lighting the carriage."

Gordon gave a little shiver. "At least I seem to have passed out before getting burned up or anything. One must be thankful for small mercies, I suppose."

"I suppose so, yes."

Long silence. Royd brooded over the print. Then Gordon said slowly:

"Doc, I'm only a human being. I just can't see a thing like this and not ask when it is going to happen. I've got to know, otherwise I'm liable to shun trains for the rest of my life! Plainly, I'm a good deal older than I am now, so—when will it happen?"

The scientist gave him a direct look. "You realize what you are asking, young man?"

"Fully! I've got to know!"

"Very well. The date when this happens will be October the nineteenth, 2019."

Gordon thought for a moment then started. "But that's only thirteen years hence! I'll only be thirty-eight!"

"Yes, I'm sorry you asked me. There it is and you cannot alter it."

"That's where you're wrong, Doc!" Gordon's face was grim. "I deliberately asked you the date so that I can sidestep it. On that date I'll lock myself in prison, go down a mine, fly to the arctic, or something. That will not come true! Not one bit of it!"

"You cannot alter time, my boy."

"I believe I can. The only reason people walk blindly into death is because they don't know when it's coming. If they did, they'd take steps to avoid it. If you knew a certain bus was going to run you down, you'd go up another street, wouldn't you?"

"I wouldn't be able. Time is written and no human power can change it. On October nineteenth, 2019, at eleven-three, you will be in that train—dead!"

Gordon was silent for a moment. "You have your

views on that, sir. I have mine."

Royd put the photographs in a new manilla folder, then placed it in the cabinet. He turned thoughtfully.

"Thank you, young man, for your co-operation. Would you care to see any intermediate scenes from your future life? Prior to the fatal date, that is."

"After what I've seen, Doc, I'd prefer to leave the whole thing severely alone—at least for the moment. You have enough proof now for any Scientific Association, surely? You can satisfy the scientists now that the 'mind reading' act isn't confined to you alone."

"You have done science an immense service. Now you will depart with your ten thousand and the inerasable memory of a certain day in 2019. I still wish you hadn't asked me to give you that date."

Gordon set his jaw. "I'm glad you did, and I've told you why. Now I'd better be going."

Nevertheless Gordon hesitated and he was not sure why. He decided that it was possibly because he had happened on to something utterly extraordinary and for that reason was loath to turn his back on it. Besides, he had somehow developed quite a regard for this pottering old genius with his Time-Camera, Scanner, or whatever he called it. That photograph of October 19, 2019, needed seeing far more than once. It needed profound study. He had to find a way to circumvent its implications.

"You hesitate, Mr. Fryer," Royd remarked. "Worried over your check? I can assure you it's quite genuine."

"I've not a second's doubt on that, sir. I'm just sort

of weighing things up. Ten thousand pounds sets me on my feet nicely, of course, and I suppose I can afford to wait for a while until something comes my way. I—I don't quite know what it is, but there is something about this place and particularly this invention of yours, which gets me. Since I'm an engineer I can appreciate your genius."

"I'm no genius, my boy: just a research scientist." Royd peered over his glasses. "You know, you've restored a lost pleasure for me and I'm very grateful. I've been stewing so long over scientific problems I had about forgotten what companionship could be like, especially the companionship of a young man who has a scientific flair as well."

Gordon began to wander, inspecting the instruments.

"I've always had the idea, Doc, that I might make something of an inventor, given the right place to settle. Tell you what: here's a proposition. Suppose I return this check, and ask you, instead, to take me on as an assistant? You could perhaps do with one?"

Royd laughed. "Do with one! I've been advertising for one for months only you probably haven't noticed. You are the ideal man for me—already proven in courage, scientific inclinations, and you're a trained engineer. What more could I ask? That is, if you're willing to tolerate a rather muddling old fool like me?"

"No muddling fool ever invented a thing like the Time-scanner! Besides I want to know more about it— in regard to my intermediate life, I mean. I also want to stand by you as living proof when you explain your theory to the scientists."

Royd rubbed his hands. "It's settled, then. As for your ten thousand pounds, that is yours—for a nerve-racking job well performed. To stand beside me I'll give you three hundred pounds a week and everything found."

Gordon spread his hands and grinned. "What could be fairer than that? That being so, I'd better depart for a moment and see if this village can supply me with some decent clothes and a laboratory smock—"

He stopped suddenly, pondering, a surprised look in his eyes.

"Well?" Royd questioned, and Gordon glanced at him sharply.

"I was just thinking, sir. That photograph you took of me as I'll be tomorrow. It showed me in here, in a smock. It looks as though it would come true."

"It will, my boy. It's inevitable."

"So it begins to appear, which makes it seem that that other date, thirteen years hence, may perhaps be—" Gordon shook his head firmly. "No! I'll find a way round that in the intervening years, even if I have to go abroad to do it!"

Royd did not say anything. His whole attitude suggested a fatalistic acceptance of immutable law.

CHAPTER TWO

BLESSINGTON EXPOSED

By evening Gordon was fully entrenched, even to having his own private sitting room and bedroom. The more he saw of the quiet grandeur of the Larches and the gentle countryside surrounding it, the more he liked it. It was as balm after the many weeks of buffeting he had endured in London when his finances had fallen to pieces,

As far as he could tell, during the quiet, informal dinner he and Dr. Royd had together, the scientist was entirely without relatives and had never married. His whole life had been devoted to obscure aspects of science, which had earned him a staggering number of degrees in which he was not remotely interested.

"Since you are satisfied with the performance of your Scanner, Doc, what comes next?" Gordon asked.

"It depends chiefly on what the Institute of Scientists will say. If this invention is approved, I shall have a busy time supervising its manufacture.... Deep down, though," Royd finished, brooding, "I think it will be rejected."

"But it can't be!" Gordon exclaimed. "You've got all

the proof you need!"

"Just so—and that's the trouble. Science admires progress, of course, but not at any price. If my invention is marketed in much the same way as an electric washer might be—which it could be because it is harmless enough to use—think of the chaos that might be started! If many of the people were able to learn the date of their death, it might put the insurance companies out of business for a start. Those with the gambling spirit could clean up illegal millions by skillfully discovering in advance the result of a certain sporting event. In the medical world, the diagnosis of supposed great specialists might be set at nought by the patient knowing he would actually live many years when only given a few months.... The more I think of it, Gordon, the less I like it.

"I begin to see that an instrument of the Scanner's capabilities could be more of a curse to Mankind than a benefit. Your own reaction showed me that. If people of the weak-minded variety start finding out when they are going to die, heaven knows where things might end. Weighing the benefits against the disadvantages, I don't feel like going any further."

Gordon frowned, turning the possibilities over in his mind. "Yes, I see your point—and maybe you're right, but it seems to me a sin that such a machine should not see the light of day."

"Oh, it will do that," Royd said. "But not, I think, as a public commodity. It could be used in the ranks of science for predicting very necessary courses of events, or for absolutely accurate weather recording, and so on. In any event, we will see how things develop. What I wish you to do in your spare time—and there will be quite a lot of it when I shall not be needing your assistance—is to develop your inventive talent. You have everything in the laboratory which you can possibly need, so turn it to account."

Gordon said: "Of course, sir, I much appreciate it. But I feel it's very one-sided. You engaged me to help you, not enjoy myself."

"And why shouldn't you enjoy yourself? You have no idea how lonely one can become just grappling with scientific problems and your domestic staff thinking you're plain crazy."

"I'll correct their views if they mention it in my hearing," Gordon promised. "For what you've done for me, I'll protect you as if you were my own father."

Royd nodded, a rather whimsical smile on his thin face. Then after thinking for a moment, Gordon asked a question.

"Regarding this 'future scanner' of yours, would you have any objection if now and again I took another look at that death-scene photo of mine?"

"None at all. It's in the second cabinet on the right, first drawer down."

"I know. I watched you put it there."

"It won't do you any good to keep studying it, Gordon. No matter what you do, or think you can do, you cannot alter what is predestined to happen."

"That depends." Gordon gave a serious smile. "You

say I can't defeat the future, but I shall.... Now, there is something else. Regarding the intermediate stages of my life, I'd rather like to see them now I've got over the first shock."

"As you wish. We can do it by degrees since you're on the premises. But don't let that invention fascinate you too much. Despite the fact that you can only live until 2019 there is much you can do before then. Let's change the subject. You say you have an inclination towards invention. Have you anything particular in mind?"

"One thing. I drafted out a sketch a long time ago. It's a watch."

Royd looked surprised. "Nothing very uncommon there."

"A watch," Gordon explained, "which is actuated by the person wearing it, designed so that the energy of the person keeps the watch always wound up. A sudden fall of energy, or maybe illness, would cause this watch to stop. Think of the benefit that would be to the medical world. They'd know the exact time when the patient started to go off the beam."

"Quite ingenious! And you think you can make this instrument?"

"In my present position, with time, money, and a laboratory, I'm sure of it. If I do, and it works, I want you to be a partner with me."

"A sleeping one if you wish, Gordon. Financially I have more money than I shall ever need— Tell you what you do. It's only half-past eight as yet. Why not go into the laboratory, and decide what you require for this watch of yours? Get yourself orientated with the place and then go to work in real earnest tomorrow? I shan't disturb you. I'm going into the library until bedtime to look up a treatise on diatoms which is bothering me."

Gordon got to his feet. "Right! What have I got to lose?"

He left the room, headed across the hall, and went into the laboratory. To commence with, he was full of resolve to check up on the materials he required for a model of his theoretical watch, but his attention kept straying to the first drawer on the second filing cabinet—and finally he could not master the temptation any longer. From the drawer he took the manilla folder and opened it, studying the photograph within.

Never in his life had he contemplated anything so earnestly, absorbing every detail, and the more he looked at it the more convinced he became that Dr. Royd had probably been right when he had said it represented the scene of a railway accident. The blurred windows, unusually bright light outside—

"I must remember never to wear a dress suit," Gordon murmured. "Nor a watch, nor a dark raglan-style coat. The fact of never wearing those things is sufficient in itself to give lie to this scene."

All of a sudden it took on a horrified aspect for him, and he pushed it hastily away in the folder again. Thereafter he did his utmost to thrust the scene out of his mind, and intently went to work upon the real purpose of his visit to this laboratory—finding the necessities for the watch he had in mind. He had just about satisfied himself that there was everything he needed when a knock on the door startled him. He put the photograph away just as Blessington, the butler, entered.

"Begging your pardon, sir—"

"Yes?" Gordon closed the filing cabinet.

"I know I have no right to say this, sir, but an inner sense tells me that I should. I don't think it wise of you to stay here as companion to a gentleman who is—er—"

"Yes?" Gordon asked again.

"I must refrain from using the exact word, sir. Surely you must have grasped that my poor master is—"

"One of the cleverest scientists of the age. Yes, I grasped that, and I'm proud to have the chance to work with him."

Blessington looked troubled. "That, sir, was not what I was going to say."

"I am aware of it." A coldness had come into Gordon's tone. "Your attitude towards your employer is entirely wrong—and it is causing him a good deal of unhappiness. Like anybody else, he resents ridicule, even if it is not openly expressed. It will have to cease."

Blessington's eyes opened a little wider in surprise. "But really, Mr. Fryer, you cannot mean that you believe in his claims? Looking into the future, for instance!"

"I believe in his claims implicitly, chiefly because he has proved them to me. If you cannot co-operate with your employer, Blessington, it seems to me there is only one answer."

Blessington stiffened, cleared his throat, and then departed without another word. Gordon settled at the bench and drew toward him some paper upon which to figure and sketch. He became so absorbed in it that he gave quite a start when the laboratory door opened and Dr. Royd came in.

"Well, well, Gordon, apparently you are a glutton for work!" he exclaimed. "It's half past eleven. As far as I'm concerned, it's time to retire. How about you?"

"Listen, Doc. I'm doing my utmost to recall the details of that watch of mine, and if I break off now I may not manage it."

"Goodnight then," the doctor said, and turned to go.

Gordon's voice stopped him. "I think you ought to know, doctor, that I have had something of a brush with Blessington, your butler. He came in here unasked and politely hinted that you are crazy. I told him what I thought about his attitude and added that if he didn't change it, there was only one alternative."

"Blessington," Royd said, "Is jealous—bitterly so—of you, Gordon. It's possible he sees in you a barrier to his own plans, and for that reason is trying to get rid of you—using the excuse of declaring me crazy and unfit to be with you for long periods."

Royd pulled up a stool and sat down. "He's a necessary evil. He holds a staff together in the house—a staff I must have if I am to be reasonably comfortable, but in return he exacts a price. Not monetary, but in the liberties he takes. I am fully aware that he has spent many nights here in this laboratory, working on a scheme of his own."

"Blessington has?" Gordon asked blankly. "But I didn't think he had a scientific idea in his head. He can't have or he wouldn't have refused to be your guinea pig."

"To be the guinea pig takes courage, Gordon. Blessington did not believe there was no risk and so refused. I don't know whether he is scientific or not, but he certainly uses this laboratory freely when he believes I am safely out of the way. I have never questioned him because I have never found anything missing or damaged. He uses my tools, I think, but not my materials. I don't want to get rid of him because he is too good a butler."

"Forgive me, sir, but I think you're making a mistake," Gordon said frankly. "No butler of mine would do as he likes without explaining himself."

"You are young and vigorous, my boy: I'm not. Blessington could put me in hospital with one blow if he wanted to."

"Possibly, but he couldn't kill you. Ninety-three, remember!"

Royd laughed a little and got up from the stool. "Anyway, there you have it. I'd suggest you let Blessington have his head. It's much simpler."

"And I think, sir, that you've got yourself a body-guard."

Royd said no more and took his departure. Gordon

put his notes in his pocket, switched off the desk light, and left the laboratory. As he crossed the hall, he caught a brief glimpse of Blessington surreptitiously watching his ascent of the stairs.

"Oh. Blessington—" Gordon stopped suddenly and looked over the handrail.

"Sir?"

"I'll have a glass of milk, please. I always do at night."

"Very good, sir. Since the staff has retired, I will bring it to your room."

"I don't need to put you to that trouble, Blessington. Just give it me here."

Tight-lipped with obvious annoyance of this variation in domestic schedule, Blessington departed—to return presently with the glass of milk on a salver. Gordon took it, drank it, and returned it.

"Thank you, Blessington. Goodnight."

"Goodnight, sir," the butler responded coldly, and Gordon went up the remainder of the stairs.

But he did not go to his room. He watched from concealment as the butler vanished again into the domestic regions to rid himself of tray and glass—and in those seconds Gordon acted swiftly. He ran down the stairs again, making no noise on the carpet, and quickly regained the laboratory. In a matter of seconds he gained a tall, half-empty storage cupboard in a corner and concealed himself within it, drawing the door shut. As he knew from earlier surveys, the door had air-holes at the top through which he could look if anything happened.

It was almost an hour later before anything did, and the sound of the laboratory door opening jerked Gordon up from his crouched position on the cupboard floor. He peered through the air-holes and saw the one central laboratory light come up. Blessington stood there, looking about him. He gazed unseeingly at the cupboard; then evidently satisfied, he moved to the workbench, pulled off his alpaca jacket, which he evidently wore when off duty and rolled up his shirt-sleeves.

Intently Gordon watched. About Blessington's shoulder was the strap of a haversack. This haversack he now unslung gently and put on the bench in front of him, taking from it what appeared to be dozens of glass marbles and put them on the workbench. In a very short time he was at work with Royd's expensive grinding and polishing machine, at times using other delicate tools to mysteriously fashion the marbles. As Royd had guessed, Blessington evidently had no designs on using his master's materials; he was working with his own stuff.

Nevertheless, it was not to be tolerated without even a by-your-leave from the master of the house. Gordon opened the cupboard door and stepped out. Blessington swung round, his eyes wide in amazement; then he hastily switched off the machine he had been oper-ating.

"Somewhat uncalled-for from a butler, Blessington, isn't it?" Gordon asked, pausing beside the bench.

Blessington's eyes glinted. "At the moment, Mr. Fryer, I'm not a butler, I'm off duty—so I don't see the need for being respectful. You're an interfering snooper!"

"Exactly. Since Dr. Royd has been kind enough to give me a chance to work with him and for him, I feel bound to protect his interests—and this sort of thing has either got to stop or be permitted by Dr. Royd himself."

"I'm not asking the master anything! It isn't safe."

"What isn't? I'm sure Dr. Royd is a reasonable man."

"In some things," Blessington admitted, hard-faced, "but because he's a scientist he'd be onto this idea of mine like a shot if he knew about it. No, thank you! I prefer to work in secret, otherwise I'd have asked for permission."

"These nocturnal operations of yours are not so secret as you imagine, Blessington. Your employer knows of them but disregards them: he told me so, and I decided to find out what you're up to."

"And what the hell does that matter to you?" Blessington snapped. "You monkey around with this equipment too, don't you? You're only a paid servant, same as I am."

"That—and a little more," Gordon answered. "I am Dr. Royd's companion, and as such his bodyguard. As long as I can stop it, I will not tolerate anything underhand going on. Explain yourself! What are you doing?"

Gordon's gaze traveled to the glass marbles and the butler put his hand over them, but not very effectively.

There were too many.

"Glass eyes!" Gordon exclaimed, surprised. "Very well made too!"

"Thanks." The butler smiled sourly. "Yes, they're glass eyes and they ought to be good, seeing that my father was one of the finest glass eye makers in the country and passed most of his knowledge on to me. But our factory was burned down and some twist in the insurance stopped us getting compensation. After that I decided to look for some kind of work where I could make enough money to revive the business. I saw a golden opportunity as butler to this crank of a Dr. Royd with his well-equipped laboratory—so I took to being a gentleman's gentleman and got away with it, chiefly because only somebody with a mighty good reason would stay with a crazy devil like him."

"Leave Royd out of this," Gordon warned. "Have you managed to restore your business?"

"I haven't had time, but I'm laying the foundations and making a good deal of money."

"I can't think how. There are several glass eye makers in the country with every facility and good connections. How can you compete with them?"

"Because this glass eye is different. It can do something that not even my father could perfect, but I've managed it with the equipment there is here. I can make a glass eye move about like a real one. None of your fixed stare to the front. The eye moves with its neighbor."

"All else apart, congratulations," Gordon exclaimed.

"I still can't think why, in the home of a great scientist, you didn't ask for permission to continue your work outside duty hours. I'm sure Dr. Royd would have given his sanction."

"No doubt—and have snooped and questioned all the time. As his butler I would have had to tell him. I'm not taking that risk. This secret belongs to me alone."

"Apparently you have little faith in your fellow men, Blessington."

"I haven't any—especially if they're scientific."

"All right," Gordon shrugged. "As Dr. Royd's assistant I'm telling you this: either ask his permission or else leave. I'll implement that in the morning. You're either a butler or a glass eye manufacturer and you can't go on working in secret."

Blessington hesitated for a moment, then he savagely scooped his glass eyes into the haversack, put it back on his shoulder, and picked up his jacket.

"I thought there'd be trouble the moment you stepped in," he said bitterly. "Evidently I was right. Very well, I quit. Tomorrow I'll tell the old man myself."

With that he left, taking care to close the door quietly despite his temper. Gordon shook his head to himself, nonetheless convinced that he had done the right thing. For the moment there seemed to be nothing for it but go to bed and wait for the storm in the morning.

Then Gordon hesitated, his glance caught by something gleaming under the slightly raised base of the nearby lathe. Raking beneath it with his pencil he brought a glass eye to view. Evidently it had rolled there when Blessington had put his hand over his prizes.

Picking up the eye, Gordon studied it carefully, trying to determine where came the trick that would make it move when in position—unless of course it was not complete. Certainly he could find no clue; but another thought stirred through his mind at the same time, quite a surprising one, one of those deep-seated conceptions, which exist only in the minds of those who are naturally inventive.

"It might work at that," he mused. "Keep this as a specimen to work on."

Pondering over the thought buzzing around in his mind he switched off the light and left the laboratory. He was still thinking deeply when he fell asleep—and at breakfast next morning he learned from Dr. Royd that Blessington had already taken his departure.

"A great pity," Royd sighed. "He was a good man. I'm afraid the rest of the domestics won't be long following his example."

Gordon shrugged. "If domestics are paid enough, sir, I should imagine they shouldn't be hard to find. Blessington left because of me. I surprised him last night monkeying about with your laboratory equipment."

"Oh?" Royd appeared mildly astonished. "What was he up to?"

"Manufacturing glass eyes—" and Gordon gave the details.

"Evidently a most distrusting man," Royd commented. "I would have given him all the facilities he needed. However, you acted right. No use having a man who is trying to do two things at once."

"I believe," Gordon said slowly, "that he gave me a great idea, which if I can develop it, will mark one of the greatest strides ever in the science of optics." From his pocket he fished the glass eye that Blessington had inadvertently left behind. "See that, Doc? Note its difference from the conventional glass eye, and see if you cannot visualize a certain great possibility."

Royd took the 'marble' in his fingers and studied it intently for a long time; then he handed it back.

"To me, it is just a glass eye of unusual design. I don't detect any 'great possibility' about it."

Gordon smiled. "Well, I do. If it works out, I'll tell you later. Otherwise I'm not going to give you the chance of calling me a chump."

On that the subject dropped, and after breakfast— Royd still being preoccupied with his diatom problem in the library—Gordon went into the laboratory to continue his detailed planning of the wonder-watch. It still had first place in his mind, despite the beginnings of another idea in connection with the glass eye.

He was in the midst of his work and stooping to his task when something occurred to him. He was exactly in the position that had been photographed the day before! It gave him a curious thrill, a shock, to observe the exact manner in which it had been foretold and come about. It made him think of another date, far away as yet—October 19, 2019.

"Plenty of time to circumvent that," he muttered, but

just the same he went to the filing cabinet to extract the photograph which had been made of today. Then he got another shock. The manilla folder was there but both photographs, of today and October 19, 2019, had vanished.

The thought that perhaps they had slipped out into the drawer occurred to him and he began a systematic search, without result. Troubled, he went in search of Royd and found him in the library with books piled up on the desk.

"I haven't taken them," Royd said finally, when he knew what had happened. "Only suggestion I can make is Blessington."

"I thought of that—but why should he? What good would they be to him?"

"No idea." Royd considered this. "Not that it matters. I can always take another one, if you wish."

Gordon was silent, trying to fathom Blessington's motive.

"Yes," he said finally, "I believe I would like another scene of that supposedly fatal day, chiefly because I think there was a mistake somewhere. What makes it so certain that it was the day of my death? Couldn't I have been unconscious, or something?"

"No; it was death. Your brain gave no reading beyond that date. Sorry, young man, but there's no sense in deluding you." Royd pushed his books on one side. "I've done all I need in here. I'll make a fresh reading."

When they had reached the laboratory Gordon asked a question: "Look, Doc, can you fine-focus this apparatus of yours so that you can take other photographs of the fatal day, immediately preceding the alleged death-scene? I'd like to find out what is supposed to lead up to it so I can avoid it. I'd like to have a few taken at random through the next thirteen years too, if I may."

Royd gave his tired smile. "Certainly. I'll start with one next week, then next year, and so on. Then I'll reproduce for a few hours before the final scene. Let's get busy, shall we?"

Gordon settled in the chair beneath the apparatus. He remained under the instrument for close on an hour, during which time Dr. Royd took half-a-dozen photographs. As the last one emerged damply from the mysterious developing tank, Gordon got up and crossed to the bench where the prints had been laid in special drying cradles. In profound interest he studied them, Royd having affixed a date to each one.

There was one of a week hence where Gordon recognized himself holding up a half-completed watch to the laboratory window.

"Evidently I'll get that far," he commented. "Good!"

The next photograph was of March 27, 2007, a year hence. It showed him in a well-cut suit in a sumptuous office. At his desk was a thin-faced man with gray hair, and apparently in a bad temper. These points Gordon passed over in his study of the young woman to whom he was talking. She was small, graceful, and blonde, with exactly the kind of face that appealed to him. Her hand was laid on his arm as though she were trying to restrain him.

"Wonder who she is?" Gordon asked, and Royd smiled.

"You'll inevitably find out a year hence. Don't start cudgeling your brains now. Meantime take a look at this: apparently the same young lady."

The third photograph was for June 10, 2010, four years hence. It showed the same girl, though obviously older, coiled up on the lawn before a stylish modern house. Nearby Gordon recognized himself, looking much fatter. He had a hand half raised in playful acknowledgment to a little girl rolling a ball on the grass. Clearly she was very young and unsteady on her feet.

"Seems self-evident," Royd commented dryly. "Evidently your future wife, Gordon."

Gordon picked up the fourth photograph. "Mmm, what's this?"

The date was September 6, 2013, seven years hence. Looking fatter than ever, Gordon beheld himself standing on a rostrum addressing an immense gathering of men and women. Around him were other men and women, looking towards him in absorbed interest. Dimly in the background hung a pennant on which were the letters B.O.A.

"What would I have to do with British Overseas Airways?" Gordon demanded, puzzled.

"Try British Optical Association. Same letters."

Gordon snapped his fingers. "That proves it, then! The idea I got about the glass eye is apparently going to work out."

He picked up the fifth photograph, and his brief satisfaction changed to grimness. It was for October 19, 2019, the fatal day, and evidently depicted a scene a few hours before his decease. It was not a pretty scene, either. In very dim light, with what appeared to be crumbling walls and distant street lamps as a backdrop, he was struggling frantically with somebody, the face of whom was just hidden by his own body. High aloft was a knife, and it gave Gordon a cold shock to discover that he was gripping it. He appeared to be wearing a black coat and homburg hat, in complete contradiction to the raglan coat depicted in the sixth photograph of the death scene.

There it was again, exactly as before. Immutable. Unchanged.

"Very interesting," he said finally. "I'm wondering who it is I'm fighting in the few hours prior to the finish."

"You're as wise as I am, my boy." Royd picked up the prints, pushed them in the folder, and then into the cabinet. "Whenever you want to look at these you know where they are. I hardly think they are likely to be taken now Blessington has gone—nor can I imagine what he wanted with the others."

Royd clapped Gordon on the shoulder.

"I'm sorry that this machine of mine is so utterly ruthless in its exposures, but that is the very nature of time and circumstance. You've shown you are not a weak character, so all I can suggest is that you enjoy what appears to be prosperity in the intervening years."

Gordon said: "I don't accept this verdict. I'll disprove an earlier scene somewhere and that will show that this ruling is not inevitable."

"As you wish.... And now what about that watch you were working on? Quite all right with me if you want to carry on with it. I've two days' work yet to do on the diatoms, and I also have to ring the Institute of Scientists concerning this brain-scanner."

Gordon nodded absently and Royd toddled from the laboratory. For a moment or two Gordon stood thinking, then by deliberate effort he forced himself away from grim speculations and turned his attention to the designs of his watch—to such good effect that he was very soon completely absorbed in his task.

But as day followed day and Dr. Royd made no demands upon him, it gradually dawned on Gordon that the agreeable old codger didn't really need help at all. All he needed was company, and having obtained it nothing else seemed to cross his mind. So Gordon found himself free to work, with the additional advantage of having a very experienced scientist on hand when he hit up against a big snag.

In two more days his plans for his watch were complete: and in four days he commenced the actual manufacture of a model. By the end of a week he had the model half completed, and for the first time, Dr. Royd saw it taking shape as he came into the laboratory.

"Very intricate, my boy," he commented, after studying the framework intently. "On what principle does it work?"

"As I mentioned earlier, body energy motivates it," Gordon responded. He picked up the watch and indicated the internal setting with an ultra-fine screwdriver. "This central spindle here projects beyond the back of the outer case and finishes in a magnetic cup which seals itself on the wrist of the wearer underneath the watch. That does two things: it makes the transmission of body energy complete, and also prevents the wearer from dislodging the watch. Once fitted in place by a technical expert, it need never be removed. It can be there until the death of the wearer, the specially devised gold wrist-strap being made to expand and contract should the wearer become fatter or thinner. Thus it will be completely dust-, damp-, and shock-proof."

"And there is no way of removing it from the wrist?"

"None, unless one files through the wrist strap. Nobody should need to, since it will be exactly fitted and as natural to the wearer as—as artificial teeth. One can wash, or bath, or go swimming without fear of harming it."

"Some may like it, some may not," Royd said. "To wear a watch until death sounds a tall order to me. Still, maybe the novelty will do it."

"I'm pinning my hopes on that. In any case nobody need be frightened off by the permanency of the watch—after all, it will file off easily enough—but it shouldn't be necessary. As to the rest—this minute transformer in the watch center steps up the energy received from the magnetic cup, and that energy is transferred to this driving spindle here. The regulation is such that as long as the wearer is in reasonably normal health, the watch will keep perfect time. I've allowed for variations in bodily metabolism, climatic conditions, and so forth. No mainspring, no hairspring—in other words, an electric clock driven by the current of a human being. It will be possible to start it off again in the event of it stopping owing to ill health, I'll see to that."

Royd nodded his approval.

"The casing," Gordon finished, holding the watch to the light of the window, "is transparent, so it can be seen if anything is radically wrong without taking the watch to bits. And that—"

He stopped, lowered his arm, and gave a curious, half-frightened glance over his shoulder.

"I—I did it!" he exclaimed, startled. "I'd made up my mind that I wouldn't, but I did. Quite unthinkingly."

"Meaning?" Royd questioned in surprise.

"The photograph, of course! One of those we took a week ago, depicting me holding a half-completed watch to the window! I'd made up my mind to disprove the Scanner and not do that—yet I did, quite unconsciously."

Dr. Royd looked over his glasses. "When you are old as I am, my boy, you'll have learned how immutable time is."

"I'll never be as old as you! That's what haunts me!"

"I'm sorry." Royd looked away. "Damned silly

remark of mine. I keep forgetting. Anyhow, carry on with your job and forget anything else, Gordon. You're doing fine. This afternoon, by the way, I'm attending a meeting of the Institute of Scientists to explain this brain-scanner of mine. Maybe you'll come along as witness?"

"Gladly."

Royd nodded and left the laboratory. Gordon worked on until lunchtime—the cook and other members of the domestic staff having decided to stay on after all—then in the afternoon the journey was made to London with the partly dismantled brain-scanner in the back of Dr. Royd's car.

* * * * * * *

Gordon found the scientific meeting impressive enough, with every member quietly attentive as Royd rambled cheerfully through the intricacies of his invention. Then, when it came to his turn to verify the old scientist's statements, Gordon promptly did so—but he felt he could not control the words that followed his corroboration.

"In the name of humanity, gentlemen, I have something to add," he exclaimed earnestly, studying the faces turned to him. "Though this machine is all that Dr. Royd claims for it—which fact can be readily proven by any of you here—I beg of you not to turn it into production. I think it might become the greatest curse known to mankind!"

Dr. Royd raised his eyebrows, and then gave a

knowledgeable smile.

"For Dr. Royd this machine presents no terror," Gordon went on. "It has even brought comfort in that he knows he will live to be ninety-three—but to me has been revealed the anguishing fact that in thirteen years I must die. Though there may be an error in the machine, though I have cheerfully told myself I will not do the things that a future scene has predicted, there is always that terrifying thought at the back of my mind that it may all come true! I shall fight it because I must—but why inflict similar suffering on countless other individuals? If they are to die tomorrow, then let them be happy today."

Gordon turned abruptly. "I'm sorry, Dr. Royd. I know all that I've said has probably undermined your chances with this venerable body. But I must say what I think."

"Of course, my boy, of course." Royd rose to his feet again as Gordon sat down. "I think, gentlemen, that in inventing the brain-scanner, I have somewhat over-reached myself, at least as far as public peace of mind is concerned, and therefore I withdraw it."

"But at least let us test it, Dr. Royd!" the Chairman entreated. "We know only too well your genius in these matters: surely you wish science to acclaim that genius?"

"Yes—I do." Royd considered and then shook his head. "But I do not wish acclaim at the expense of people's peace of mind. To prove the machine's power somebody must test it—and that somebody may be put in precisely the same plight as my young friend Gordon Fryer. Consider how merciless the machine is. One cannot even commit suicide to escape the fate it has ordained, because whatever date it reveals is absolutely true and cannot be altered.... No, gentlemen, one sufferer is enough. If you care to make trivial mention of my researches into the human brain, I shall consider myself repaid. Thank you for your attention."

What followed was very close to uproar, but Dr. Royd remained adamant. Fifteen minutes later he and Gordon were on their way back to Nether Bolling with the apparatus once more in the rear of the car.

Gordon said: "Sorry, sir, for upsetting things like that. If you'll just allow me to finish that watch of mine I'll clear out. I'm going to be a jinx as far as you're concerned."

"On the contrary, you've made me consider something which never occurred to me before. I'd never thought that there could be scientific achievement which, though appearing beneficial, could bring such unhappiness to the human race. I don't want any part of such conceptions. As for your leaving, I won't hear of it."

The remainder of the journey back to Berkshire was covered mainly in silence, and during it Dr. Royd seemed to arrive at some important decision. The nature of it became apparent when Gordon had helped him to replace the scanner in the laboratory.

"Don't bother bolting it down," Royd said, as Gordon looked for the spanner to tighten the floor bolts.

"No? Bit it won't hold like that—"

"I don't wish it to. I have an alteration to make. Give me the spanner, please."

Gordon handed it over, one of the big adjustable variety, then before he could anticipate anything Royd had driven the heavy tool straight into the central mechanism of his Time Scanner. The casing split instantly, releasing a multitude of fine wires, broken glass, and jagged pieces of insulation.

"That feels better," Royd said, tossing the spanner down.

"But—" Gordon stared aghast. "Do you realize what you've done, sir? That marvelous machine of yours! You've ruined it!"

"Exactly." Royd was quite complacent about the incident. "And now I'm going to destroy all my notes concerning it. Some things are too good to be true, Gordon, and this instrument was one of them. I've seen the mental torture it can produce to know the future—with you as the guinea-pig—and I don't intend to spread the diabolical possibilities any further."

On the face of things there was nothing Gordon could do. He looked at the shattered instrument in despair, and for a while played around with the broken entrails—but finally he had to give it up. He hadn't the remotest idea how to fit the thing together again. Not that it would have done any good if he had, for Royd was obviously determined to disavow the whole business.

Such seemed to be the case, for beyond remarking

at the evening meal that he had burned all his notes on the scanner, he did not again refer to the matter. He made his statement without rancour, evidently quite sanguine in his own mind that he had made the best move possible.

Gordon, for his part, could not help but think that he was himself personally responsible for causing Royd to destroy his wonderful handiwork, even though it was plain Royd himself did not look at it in this light. The only thing Gordon could think of to make matters square with his benefactor was to complete the watch and have Royd share in the credit for having provided the wherewithal to make the watch possible. And in two more weeks the watch was completed. Gordon held it up proudly for Royd to see as the old man pottered about the laboratory doing various routine jobs.

"Finished and perfect!" Gordon announced in triumph. "The transparent casing as hard as tungsten and completely sealed, the edges bound with gold—and a gold strap. And here is the adjustment lever for regulation. I'd like you to wear it for me, sir, to test it."

"I?" Royd repeated. "But surely you would prefer to carry out the test for yourself?"

"I'd like to, yes, but I've taken a vow never to wear a wrist watch. According to schedule I'll be found dead with a watch on my wrist and that's something I'm going to defeat."

"But, my dear boy, the watch in the photograph is nothing like this. You've nothing to fear."

"Maybe not, but I'd prefer you wore it. If it works as

I think it will, I'll make another one and then we'll see if we can get a watch manufacturer interested."

Royd smiled. "Very well. But remember, as far as a manufacturer is concerned, the credit for this watch is yours. I shall merely testify as to its efficiency."

"I would like it to be more than that," Gordon said seriously. "But for you I couldn't have manufactured the thing anyway. I want your name to be connected with it. It will carry more weight, too. I'm unknown, but you are not."

"There has to be a beginning for all of us."

"Not for me. I'm not anxious to begin because I'll have to stop so soon. Won't you please allow me to call this the 'Royd Energy Watch'? The name will do it."

"If it will give you any pleasure, yes," the scientist answered, surprised. "But how are you going to explain it is your invention and then have my name on it?"

"I shall explain it as being your invention, I being only a high pressure agent for you."

"Oh! I see. You wouldn't be doing this because of some mistaken idea about recompense for the Time Scanner would you?"

"I would. After all, I did ask you to be my partner."

Royd shrugged. "Very well. Your interests have become mine, Gordon, as you know. Put the watch on my wrist and let's see what happens."

"You realize, that when I do, you'll need a file to take it off again?"

"Certainly. And only a desperate measure will make me want to do that. As you see, I have a signet ring that I have worn for over fifty years. There isn't much difference if it's comfortable enough."

Gordon turned, picked up the watch from the bench and carefully arranged the magnetic pad so it leeched tightly to Royd's wrist. Then he snapped the gold bracelet into position, the links locking themselves immovably into place.

"Excellent," Royd smiled, "and as comfortable as an old shoe! Going, too!" He watched the central sweep hand moving smoothly round the white dial. "Obviously, Gordon, I was not mistaken in you when I gave you time to think and work."

"I'm not so sure about that, sir. But for me you would not have destroyed the Scanner. Anyhow, to get back to business: wear the watch for the next few days and we'll see how it goes on. Meantime I'll make another to show our prospect."

"Thought of anybody in particular?" Royd asked.

"Yes—Irwin's of Sheffield. About the biggest watch-makers in the country, and always bringing out new gadgets. This notion ought to get them by the ears."

Royd nodded and thrust his hands in his jacket pockets whilst he considered. Then in some wonder he withdrew his right hand, holding a letter therein. He gave a guilty start.

"Why, of course! So sorry, Gordon, I should have given you this letter earlier. Johnson—the maid who is taking Blessington's place for the moment—gave it to me to give to you. It came by special messenger just after breakfast."

"Oh?" Puzzled, Gordon took the envelope and studied the handwriting. It was neat and upright and entirely unfamiliar to him. Quickly he thumbed open the envelope and then stared fixedly at the square piece of card he withdrew.

"I'll be a—" he began, then stopped. Royd, who had politely turned aside, turned back again.

"Anything wrong?"

"I don't know about wrong, sir, but certainly a confounded mystery. Take a look."

Royd contemplated the card and then frowned. The card had typewritten characters and said simply:

> The Date is October 19, 2019. Don't ever forget it! Just consider this as a reminder!

"Somebody," Royd said, "has a pretty vindictive sense of humor, and I can think of only one person—Blessington! He was the only one who knew of the experiments I was conducting."

Gordon's eyes narrowed. "I believe you're right! Now I begin to see why he took those photographs. The death scene might be of value to him even if the other was not."

"Of value? In what way?"

"Blessington," Gordon said, "is quite one of the most perverted men I ever met. There are vicious depths in him, which make me crawl when I think about them. I could tell from the way he looked at me on the night I found him in the laboratory that if he could ever pay me out for queering his chances, he would. Now he's started doing it."

"As I grow older I grow denser," Royd sighed. "I just don't see the point."

"Don't you realize what sort of a mental stab a note like this gives me? Imagine it later on, if it ever gets that far—warning me how many days I have left! Slow, insidious mental poison! I'll gamble this is the opening gambit of a war Blessington intends to wage against me, unless I can find a way to stop him. I can't have the law on him for poison-pen tactics or blackmail because all he is doing is stating a truth."

Royd rubbed his chin. "I can see all that, but how does he know the date of your death? It wasn't on the photograph."

"A man like Blessington would have been listening at the door: that doesn't puzzle me for a moment." Gordon picked up the discarded envelope. It bore the London postmark.

"Which doesn't help much," Royd commented. "In a small town we might have a chance of tracing him, but in London he's lost in the mass. Oh, take no notice!" he added, smiling. "A childish game like this isn't even worth considering!"

"As it stands it certainly isn't, but if Blessington goes on doing it I'll have to find a way to deal with him. I can't stand a state of never being allowed to forget!"

Royd hesitated for a moment and then said quietly: "Better get busy with your second wrist-watch, Gordon. Take your mind off other things."

Gordon nodded, conscious of the wisdom of the

suggestion. And as on the previous occasion, he managed to be as preoccupied in his task that the shadow looming over him did not gain much occupancy in his thoughts.

CHAPTER THREE
UNEXPECTED VISITOR

In another week the second watch was completed and a journey to Irwin's of Sheffield followed. The managing director, a bluff, gray-haired man, readily granted an interview.

After he had heard an explanation of the watch, Charles Irwin said: "Sounds to me, gentlemen, as though you have something." Royd held out his wrist and Irwin watched the hour hand on its endless journey. Then he took the duplicate watch which Gordon handed to him and studied its transparent case against the light.

Irwin said: "I shall ask my experts to examine this and report to me—but from what I can see, given the right advertising, you have an idea here which will sweep the country—and eventually the world. I think the public may shy at the title of 'Royd Energy Watch', so I suggest we call it the 'Forever Watch'. How's that?"

"You know more about advertising than we do, Mr. Irwin," Royd smiled. "By all means. Eh, Gordon?"

Gordon nodded. "Just as long as Dr. Royd gets the credit for it. That's all I ask—as his agent. Very well then, Mr. Irwin, the watch is yours for examination and patent rights have already been filed for your protection and ours. When may we expect to hear something from you?"

"In about a week."

But Gordon's jubilation was cut short when, with Royd, he returned to the Larches. For another letter had arrived in the interval.

As before it was typewritten, addressed to Gordon, and postmarked London. Savagely he ripped the envelope and then took forth the solitary card from within. It said:

> Thirteen years is not such a very long time when you come to think of it!

Gordon gave a grim look as Royd glanced over the card. Then he handed it back.

"Definitely Blessington," he said. "If he means to keep this up for thirteen years it's going to cost him a fortune in stamps! The man's an idiot."

Gordon tore the card savagely in pieces and flung them in the hall wastepaper basket. Then he said slowly: "I think I ought to get away from here, sir. The change of address will not be known to Blessington, and if he sends anything further I shan't be here to receive it. Naturally you won't send them on to me."

"Sheer defeatism, boy!" Royd shook his head. "Better to tear these letters up unread than have their contents disrupt your mind. Even if you did run for it you can be sure that Blessington would find you.

Forget it and stay here."

Gordon sighed. "Yes, you're probably right, sir. It would be damned selfish of me to run, too. I don't think you'd be able to survive long without my companionship and that would mean you'd have to uproot yourself and chase after me. You must excuse my saying this, but you have come to depend on me a great deal."

"I'm afraid you're right," Royd admitted, smiling.

So, for the moment, there seemed to be nothing else for it, as far as Gordon was concerned, but to stay exactly where he was. It was too late that evening to do any more work in the laboratory—developing the theory he had devised concerning the Blessington glass eye—so instead he spent it working on his notes in the library whilst Royd—also in the library—covered several sheets of paper with notations concerning diatoms.

"I'm not at all sure about the fluid I've worked out for these things," he murmured, half to himself—and Gordon glanced up.

"What things, Doc?"

"The diatoms. I have a considerable number of them stored in the laboratory—microscopic algae in a solution of sodium chloride at the moment. I've been casting around for a different medium in which to put them."

"Might I ask why? At the moment I haven't the vaguest idea as to the nature of your experiments."

Royd smiled apologetically. "No, of course you haven't. What I am trying to do is find a way to regulate growth during the period of evolution from birth to maturity. Diatoms—the simplest form of life—afford the best subjects for experiment. I am seeking an external solution which, reacting directly on the outer cells instead of through the glands, will produce growth and development beyond the average. In other words, I am looking for a wonder-lotion which will make the future races of Mankind supermen and superwomen."

"Never stop trying to improve on Nature, do you?" Gordon smiled. "If you're not probing into the future, you're trying to make it better. As I see it, then, you want a solution to react on the outer cells in such a way as to build them up?"

"Exactly. The one I have worked out—the culture as I call it—is not too good. I think I'll have to try a secondary one first. Maybe you'd care to watch? I'm going to test it now. Basic Fluid X-nineteen and Reagent Forty-two."

Gordon promptly accompanied the old scientist from the library and into the laboratory, thereafter watching the preparation of Basic Fluid X/19. Of what it was composed Royd did not say, but it had a deep ruby color. Reagent 42 was plainly and simply water with a dash of some lemon-tinted chemical.

"Now," Royd said. "Let us see."

He swiftly poured the reagent into the basic fluid that lay half-filling a big transparent container like a goldfish bowl. When the two liquids met each other, there was a mysterious surging and steaming and a brief uprush of pleasant-smelling vapor.

"Let's see how our diatoms behave in this," Royd said, and crossed to one of the huge ventilated cabinets in which he kept specimens. Gordon kept his eyes on the bowl of liquid and casually lighted one of the cigarettes his nervous tension had lately caused him to resume smoking—and it was on that instant that the world seemed to come to an end.

There was a stupendous bang, as though a thunderbolt had landed right in the laboratory. A flash of vivid white flame followed and then acrid black smoke curled into the polished ceiling. Neither Gordon nor Royd were in any way hurt, but their hearts were definitely hammering with shock. Blankly they stared at the bowl where the mystery liquid should have been. But it was not there anymore, and the bowl had been smashed into a thousand pieces.

Gordon laughed uneasily and ground his heel upon the still smoldering cigarette on the floor.

"I'm afraid that was my fault, sir. I lighted my cigarette, but I'd no idea that stuff was inflammable."

"Neither had I!" In wonder Royd went to the bench. "Of all the extraordinary things! The stuff just blasted out of existence—not even a trace of dampness. It must have a terrific volatility."

"Just as well you didn't put your precious diatoms in it. It would have killed them."

The diatomic experiment seemed to have gone completely from Royd's mind. His eyes were thoughtful as he took down two jars of liquid—one the Basic

Fluid X/19 and the other Reagent 42. Very carefully he distilled a small quantity of each into a beaker and then, stepping to a distance, he struck a match and tossed it forward. Exactly a similar result as before was obtained, but on a smaller scale. An explosion, a flash, and a cloud of dispersing smoke.

"Petrol is plain water compared to this!" Gordon cried. "What on earth is it?"

Royd rubbed his hands gently together and chuckled. "My boy, by the sheerest accident we've hit upon something of importance—maybe vast importance! We must investigate further. We have here a liquid so highly volatile that—as you remarked—it puts ordinary spirit in the shade. Let me think now: the Basic Fluid is distilled from ammonia and thinned with an extract of Z/29. It costs me about a pound for ten gallons. Couldn't be cheaper."

Gordon began to behold vast possibilities. "And the reagent? It's water, isn't it, with something added?"

"Not ordinary water," Royd corrected. "Heavy water, on which so many scientists have experimented with varying results. It has more atoms in its constitution than ordinary aquapura. There is something added, yes—Formula Eight, making use of a liquid extract from a mineral belonging as eighty-five in the Periodic Table, one of the missing elements not properly relegated to science. I found it long ago. It melts easily and produces a pale yellow liquid. I call it Roydium. Not that any of that matters," Royd went on intently. "We have something here, Gordon, as big and bigger than that wonder watch of yours. We must make tests again and again until we're sure."

"And then?"

"Then if it's all we think it is, you'll offer it to the best and biggest chain of garages in Britain as a substitute for petrol."

"And I can see the big oil companies letting me get away with that!" Gordon exclaimed.

"They won't—which is just the point. They should make you a tremendous offer to suppress the stuff. That ought to set you on your feet for good, along with the watch."

Gordon frowned. "But where do you come into this, sir? It isn't my discovery."

"On the contrary. If you hadn't lighted your cigarette, it wouldn't have been discovered at all."

"I know, but the formulae belong to you. I couldn't—"

"You could, and you shall." Royd was entirely firm. "You allowed me to take the credit for a watch I didn't invent, and I have felt guilty about it ever since. Here is my chance to repay you. Say no more about it. We'll give this stuff a thorough testing—preferably in my own car. First thing tomorrow morning."

"Okay!" Gordon answered. "As this is a partnership it doesn't matter who invents what!"

So at eleven o'clock the following day Gordon had the car ready for the test, the fuel tank drained. It was refilled with the mystery liquid—at a ridiculous cost compared to that of ordinary motor spirit, and thereupon the test began. Possibly no test of a fuel had ever been made so easily, or produced such amazing results. Though Gordon took the car for a hundred-mile jaunt he returned with the tank still nearly full, so high was the volatility of the mystery liquid.

"By accident," Royd said slowly, his eyes bright behind his spectacles, "we have happened upon the most powerful fuel ever known! And by far the least expensive. Any chemist can make it, which does away with freight charges, tankers, and imports from foreign lands. It's time we got this marketed!"

No further time was wasted. A gallon of the stuff was made up, named 'Spiritine,' and taken to the head-quarters of British Garages, the largest fuel concern in the country and suppliers of motor spirit to over three thousand garages and drive-ins.

"To me," the managing director said dubiously, "it all sounds highly improbable. In fact, gentlemen, we have on many occasions had inventors here with magic cubes, tabloids, and liquids which they claim can take the place of petrol—"

"Take this," Gordon interrupted quietly, handing over the gallon tin. "Drain a car tank of its petrol and use this in its place. The result will amaze you."

Gordon had made a profound understatement. After a test the managing director returned to the office with a completely transformed expression.

"Mr. Fryer," he said, "you are to be congratulated. What a discovery! What a motor spirit! Gentlemen, this Spiritine of yours will completely revolutionize the petroleum industry!"

"One day," Royd said, "reserves of petroleum will come to an end. This never will. As Mr. Fryer has told you, any chemist can make up the formula. All that is needed are laboratories for the distillation of the fuel."

"Exactly. An astounding discovery! Mr. Fryer, you will wish to come to some financial arrangement. We will, the moment my chemists have checked the stuff and proved it is all you claim."

"That," Gordon said, acting the part which Royd had prearranged for him, "chemists cannot do. There are ingredients in this fuel that no ordinary chemist will be able to analyze. There is even part of an element which is not in the Periodic Table."

"Periodic Table?" the managing director looked puzzled. "What is that? I'm an executive, not a scientist."

"In which case you wouldn't understand," Royd smiled.

"Then where are we?" the managing director asked. "We naturally cannot pay for something without knowing what it is."

"We do not expect you to," Gordon said. "I believe you have a certain number of garages with a spare tank, in case of an emergency?"

"Certainly. Practically every garage is fitted with one. Why?"

"I suggest you select half a dozen of your best-paying garages and put up a sign for Spiritine, selling at a quarter the cost of normal fuel. We will see that the tanks in the half-dozen garages are filled. For this initial facility of publicizing our product and using your tanks and garages, we're prepared to split 50-50 on the returns. I'll sign an agreement to that effect now, if it interests you. It will be for a period of four weeks only. At the end of that time I hope we'll be on such a firm footing that we can come to some definite long-standing agreement."

"You will provide the spirit?"

"Providing you have the tanker lorries call for it at laboratories I'll name later."

The managing director did not hesitate. "I'd be a fool to turn down that suggestion," he declared. "It costs us nothing beyond some advertising and running tankers to the laboratories. Providing you make them within the London area, I agree. I'll have the agreement drawn up immediately."

He pressed a desk button and dictated to the secretary who answered his summons.

This done, he said: "Again, I say, gentlemen, that you are to be congratulated. However, there may be trouble in time with the big oil people. Had you thought of that?"

Gordon nodded. "Naturally. What of you? Are you tied to them to sell only their products and nothing else?"

"No—otherwise I couldn't have done anything. We are independent and can sell as we choose. Incidentally, I rather admire the way you hang on to your formula. Very wise."

"One has to be," Gordon said.

"Dr. Royd, I understand you are a research scientist. I assume you had something to do with this fuel invention?"

"In a modest way, yes," Boyd admitted. "The credit belongs to my young friend here. I shall remain on the directive side, making sure that no laboratory has enough knowledge to piece together the entire formula."

The secretary returned with the completed agreement. The signing of it, and the promise on Gordon and Royd's part to return within a month to survey developments, ended the matter. The necessary instructions concerning the laboratories at which tankers must call would follow as quickly as possible.

Gordon said as they drove back toward Nether Bolling with Spiritine in the tank: "I wish you hadn't smashed up that Scanner of yours, sir; I'd rather like to have seen how this business will work out."

Royd smiled. "Recalling the increase in your waistline in future photographs, and the luxurious surroundings of what you will later call your home, I think you can look forward to success, my boy. Even without such foreknowledge, I can't see how such a product could miss. This happening, together with the possibilities of your watch can—"

"The watch! Believe it or not I'd almost forgotten about it in the general excitement. There must be something about that house of yours which promotes bright ideas."

"Not all of them are bright," Royd sighed. "The

conception of the Scanner was the worst—or at least the most dangerous—which I ever had."

To this Gordon made no comment. Indeed, he was feeling so well pleased with himself over the successful launching of both the wonder watch and the fuel scheme that the 'cloud, no bigger than a man's hand' was not disturbing him at the moment. After all, there were thirteen years to go, and in that time he would probably have found a way to prove the Scanner wrong.

In any case, in the time that followed, he had little chance to brood over the future: the present was far too interesting. Next day he spent his time helping Dr. Royd to contact the various laboratories who would create differing parts of Spiritine from the particular formula given to them. All told, Royd used six laboratories, all of them willing to give him immediate attention, because his famous name and financial standing demanded it. The tanker lorries could pick up the liquid and transfer it to the places and in the quantities specified in the contract. The actual mixing of ingredients would thereby be accomplished almost automatically and no laboratory could have a complete grasp of the entire process.

Hardly had this been arranged than news came from the managing director of Irwin's that he was ready to negotiate for exclusive handling of the 'Forever Watch' on a percentage and royalty basis. These details were promptly completed, and manufacturers, again selected by Royd, were set to work on mass production.

For the first time in his life Gordon began to feel,

when all these things were launched, that he was commencing to amount to something—then came another of those letters, which promptly threw him into black depression again. He hesitated whether or not to throw the envelope away unopened, but a certain morbid curiosity got the better of him and made him look at the card inside. This time it simply contained the date: October 19, 2019. For a while he was filled with the urge to drive into east London, from which region the letter had been postmarked, and turn everything upside down in an effort to find his tormentor—then he dismissed such an impossible notion and threw the card away. He had more things to do than heed these notes. Go one higher! That was the answer. Use Blessington's glass eye as the springboard for something to out-Blessington Blessington.

"Begging your pardon, sir—"

Gordon turned on his way to the laboratory bench and saw the general servant in the laboratory doorway.

"Yes, Ellen, what is it?"

"There's a Miss Haslam of the *Weekly Record* to see you."

"Oh? Show her in then, please. In here." The maid departed and presently ushered in a young woman who was small, vivacious and very blonde, with just the kind of features that Gordon liked. He gazed at her fixedly as she came forward, moving youthfully in her neat gray two-piece.

"Mr. Fryer?" she enquired, extending her hand.

"Yes." Gordon returned the handshake and motioned

somewhat woodenly to a chair. "Do sit down, Miss Haslam."

"Thank you." She settled and then looked at him in vague surprise, her hazel eyes wide. "I'm not interrupting anything, am I?"

"No, no, you're not interrupting anything." Gordon gave a vague smile and still stared at her. "I—er—had the impression for a moment that I'd seen you somewhere and I was just trying to recall where. Forgive my staring at you so rudely."

The girl laughed. "Of course! Though I did rather wonder. You must be confusing me with somebody else, though. I am not celebrated enough to be publicized, and I have certainly never interviewed you before."

"Just the same, I've seen you before. In a photograph."

"Really?" Miss Haslam gave a wondering look. "Anyhow, Mr. Fryer, I'm here to get some particulars about this Spiritine you've put on the market. It is being given very wide publicity by British Garages."

"Yes, so I believe." Gordon got a grip on himself—by no means an easy job. The sudden arrival of the girl whom the Scanner had indicated was to become his wife demanded an immense mental readjustment. He had not expected her for another eleven months. The fact that there must be a lead-up to the as yet unsolved incident in an unknown office on March 27, 2007, had never occurred to him.

"Do you believe," the girl asked, obviously puzzled

by his faraway manner, "that Spiritine will take the place of ordinary fuel for aircraft and motor cars?"

"I'm hoping so." Gordon sat down and behaved as rationally as he could. "Dr. Royd and I worked out the details between us and the rest is up to the public. We expect trouble with the oil companies, but we're ready for them."

"Yes, I see." Miss Haslam was scribbling in shorthand on her notepad. "Will you form a Spiritine Corporation or anything like that?"

"Too early to say, I'm afraid."

"Could you give me the background of your life? We know all about Dr. Royd from official files, but you are not recorded at all."

Gordon smiled wryly. "Normally I'm an engineer, but a series of circumstances brought me here, and I owe everything to Dr. Royd's endless generosity and assistance."

The girl shorthanded some more and then looked up again.

"I believe you are also connected with a new sort of watch? The 'Forever Watch' being put out by Irwin's. Is it yours, or Dr. Royd's?"

"Dr. Royd's. I'm only the agent for it...." Gordon broke off as Dr. Royd himself came shambling in. He half started to say something and then stopped, peering hard over his spectacles.

"Good gracious me!" he exclaimed.

Miss Haslam's expression changed. "I am wondering," she said, "what there is about me which seems to cause you gentlemen such consternation? Good morning, Dr. Royd," she finished coldly. "I recognize you from your photographs in our files. I am Virginia Haslam of the *Weekly Record*."

Royd shook hands and glanced under his eyes at Gordon.

"I won't disturb you, Gordon. I was only going to check up on a little matter concerning Spiritine, but it can wait." He hesitated, then added: "If Miss Haslam has a good deal to discuss, why not do it properly over lunch in town?"

Gordon snapped his fingers. "Darned good idea! I'm all misty-minded this morning. Can you spare the time, Miss Haslam?"

Her smile was sufficient, as far as Gordon was concerned.

In a matter of minutes he was out of his laboratory smock and escorting the girl to the garage. Ere long he was driving down the leafy lanes en route for Reading—the nearest town—the girl beside him.

"This car is traveling on Spiritine," he said. "Notice the difference? You can say in your article that you have actually ridden in a car which uses the wonder spirit."

"I should have said that in any case as part of the build-up, but forgive my saying it, Mr. Fryer, there's something about you which I don't understand. You are somehow—er—difficult to analyze."

"Oh? Maybe because I'm preoccupied."

"No, it isn't just that. It's as though you regard me not

just as a reporter but as somebody with whom you've long been acquainted."

Gordon was silent, wondering about the possibilities of so-called feminine intuition; then at last Virginia gave a shrug.

"I don't know what it is, and probably it doesn't matter, anyway. After all, I'm a reporter, not a psychoanalyst."

"Whilst we're on our way," Gordon said, "you might as well make a note of the various things you wish to ask me, then over lunch I'll do my utmost to answer your questions."

Virginia nodded almost dutifully and did exactly as she had been told. Whilst she did so Gordon studied her out of the corner of his eye. What he saw confirmed his opinion that she was a highly delectable girl. Practical, bright in manner, good-looking, good figure. Then he recalled a date thirteen years hence, and also remembered a vow he had made to himself. The sooner he started to prove that the Scanner had been wrong, the better. No surer way of doing that than cutting Virginia Haslam out of his life completely, then she could not possibly appear on the due date of March 27, 2007, a year hence.

Gordon sighed. To cut a girl like Virginia out of his life would be the hardest thing ever. Might strengthen his character, perhaps, but at the moment he was not vitally anxious to be a strong, silent man.

"I think," he said, when he and Virginia were in the corner of a cozy restaurant at the close of their lunch, "that these details I have given you will have to suffice, Miss Haslam. Henceforth I'm going to have so much to do I shan't be able to spare any time for reporters."

"That's such a pity!" She gave him a despondent glance. "I'd hoped for an exclusive series about you and that would have meant a byline for me."

"Byline?"

"Uh-huh. 'Contemporary Famous People,' by Virgie Haslam. I get paid a lot more when I have my name attached. Surely you can find a little time, Mr. Fryer? It would mean an awful lot to me. I've far too much material for just one column about you, and yet not enough for a series of articles. My editor has the fond hope that I'm getting an exclusive about you."

Gordon kept his face turned. "I'm not important enough to rate a series of articles, surely?"

"My editor thinks you are, and I do, too. Come now, please don't walk out on me at this stage!"

"Well, I—you see, there's a reason." Gordon hesitated "I've a lot of work to do for one thing, and for another I—I—don't get on very well with women. They are a disturbance to an inventor, especially when they're good-looking."

Virginia laughed shortly. "I suppose that is intended as a compliment, even if it is inside out! Don't let my dazzling beauty cramp your style, Mr. Fryer. I'm simply a business woman earning a living—and I unashamedly admit I am anxious to pump you dry of information. Fair enough?"

"Yes, but—"

"Mr. Fryer." Her hand rested gently on his. It was cool and well manicured, he noticed. "Mr. Fryer, you wouldn't spoil my hopes of a byline, would you?"

Gordon took himself in hand and rose to his feet. "Miss Haslam, I've given all the information I intend to give. I'm very sorry about your byline, but I must ask you not to bother me again."

"Oh, very well." Virginia got up and made preparations for departure.

"I'd like to drive you back to Nether Bolling," Gordon said.

"Would you?" Her eyes were scornful. "I'm perfectly capable of finding my way to the railway station, thank you!" And she walked out.

Gordon dropped his hand and his lips tightened. He watched the girl leave the restaurant and the swing doors shut behind her trim figure. He sat down again slowly and scowled.

"No worse than having a tooth out," he mused. "Hurts for the moment, but you soon forget. Anyway, I've proved the Scanner wrong," he muttered. "After that brush-off she'll certainly never have any more dealings with me—" Then he paused, conscious of a damnable paradox. For, if he had proved the Scanner to be wrong, he would not die in thirteen years' time, and that being so, he should have been nice to Virginia and asked her—after time—to marry him.

"Blast!" he growled, then motioned the waitress for his check.

He drove back to Nether Bolling in a decidedly ill

humor. Dr. Royd, back again on his diatomic experiments, was in the laboratory and immediately noticed Gordon's change of mood.

"Anything the matter, Gordon?" he enquired.

"In one sense, yes; in another, no. Anyhow I've proved the Scanner to be wrong."

"In what way?" Royd looked astonished.

"I suppose you recognized that girl as the one I'm with in an office a year hence? Well, that's one scene that won't come true! I as good as insulted her to her face so as to be rid of her. She won't come within miles of me in future."

"That," Royd said, shaking his head, "does not disprove the scanner. All you've done is make yourself miserable."

"Well, we'll see. I'm convinced I've wiped Miss Virginia Haslam out of the reckoning."

"Did you want to do that?"

"The last thing I wanted. It hurt like quicklime. She's the kind of girl I've always dreamed about—but I'm more anxious to disprove my destiny than I am to fall in love with her."

Royd sighed. "And very useless. You'll come together again inevitably. You'll see."

Gordon turned away impatiently. "I'll freshen up, Doc, and see you later."

He left the laboratory, cursing himself and mankind under his breath; but when he returned he was calmer and more content to leave it to time to prove whether or not he really had altered the course of things. As collectedly as possible he set to work on the task he had been about to start when Virginia Haslam had walked into his life—the task of making certain innovations to the Blessington glass eye.

Royd, still busy with his diatomic tests, did not speak until Gordon asked him a question.

"What did you decide to do about your diatoms in the finish, Doc?"

"I used the first fluid I thought of and now I'm waiting to see what reactions I get. In any event this task may be one of years and is merely to occupy my time. We're liable to have plenty to do in other directions if the 'Forever Watch' and Spiritine sell as we hope."

Gordon nodded and went on with his work. As usual he slowly lost himself in absorption, working with the various tools and machines the laboratory possessed, until at length Royd came and stood beside him, looking at the dismantled glass eye on the velvet square. The glass marble had been neatly bisected to disclose minute inner workings, invisible from the outside because of polarizing glass sheathing.

"Just how Blessington makes these eyes turn in the socket has me beaten," Gordon confessed. "Unless this is not a complete eye— Anyhow, that doesn't signify. I intend to go one better, devise my own method of making the eye movable—and also do something else."

"What?" Royd asked curiously.

"Create an eye that can see," Gordon answered quietly. "The one thing which science has not yet been able to do. We have false teeth, false hair, false limbs—

and in some cases even false hearts. But false eyes have been out of reach—until looking at this glass eye of Blessington's gave me the idea."

"So that was what you meant when you asked me if I could not see a great possibility in the eye?"

"Yes. This glass eye is unique in that its artificial pupil expands and contracts like a camera lens under the stimulus of light or lack of it. It occurred to me that if a light-sensitive wire were carried from the center of the artificial pupil, duplicating the normal optic nerve, and were then linked up by a surgeon to the appropriate brain ganglia, the nervous excitation known as sight ought to be produced."

Royd whistled softly. "I do believe you're right! It never dawned on me, and I can't think why it shouldn't have. But you'll need a remarkably sensitive type of wire. It will mean gathering all the visual images on to the point of the wire—a microscopic field in which to work."

"I know." Gordon became thoughtful. "I've been working on that. I may replace the pupil with a lens, conical shape, the tip of the cone turning inwards, and to which the tip of the wire will be attached."

Royd pondered for a while and then said: "You may not be aware of it, boy, because the thing is so natural to you—but you are showing yourself one of the greatest scientific geniuses since the time of Edison and Marconi. First that watch, and now this eye—I shall never cease to be grateful for the day that I had enough confidence in you to give you the run of my home and laboratory. Eventually you are going to prove a world benefactor."

"To die at thirty-eight," Gordon said, smiling bitterly. "A wonderful recompense, is it not?"

"We are not the arbiters of our own destiny, Gordon. So long as we do as much good as we can whilst we can, we shall at least make the world better for having been here."

Gordon's smile faded a little and he became thoughtful; then with a sigh he turned back to his task, struggling with all the mental power he possessed to rid himself of the shadow which had already slightly deepened across a career which promised to be brilliant.

CHAPTER FOUR

VIRGINIA INTERVENES

For Gordon there followed a month of intensive work on his research into a seeing eye. The days were so crowded with experiment, in which Dr. Royd lent a hand, and also his great scientific experience, that both men were surprised to find that the time was up for the first returns on Spiritine—a fact of which the managing director of the British Garages promptly reminded them.

To Gordon and Royd it meant deserting fascinating work for a time to attend to this other interest, but it had to be done. The managing director of British Garages could be forgiven his vague bewilderment at the apparent apathy of the two men in his office.

"I tell you, gentlemen, it's a world-beater!" he exclaimed. "At first the public was a bit wary of trying something new, but once the idea caught on Spiritine vanished like water down a sluice. I've heard rumors that the aviation companies will be getting in touch with you next. As for petrol, sales must have about hit bottom in this area."

"Not enough yet to cause the big companies any

concern," Gordon said. "They'll start sitting up when Spiritine is sold everywhere."

"Our contract has expired, gentlemen," the managing director said. "So what do we do next?"

"Renew it for twelve months on the same terms, but this time sell it to every garage you've got," Gordon replied. "We've made a start. More publicity is needed. At the end of the year we ought to be able to do something really big."

"And if the Airlines interest themselves?"

"They will be asked to wait twelve months. You have the exclusive right to sell Spiritine during that period."

The managing director looked puzzled. "Naturally, the plan will be of vast benefit to British Garages," he said, "but surely, from the business angle, you'd do far better to float your own company? You'd make a fortune in no time."

"Probably so," Gordon agreed, "but neither Dr. Royd nor I have the time for that at the moment. We're busy on a vital experiment. In twelve months our time may be easier, and in the meantime you will have done the publicizing for us."

That Spiritine could possibly be of secondary interest to its discoverers was obviously something the managing director could not understand—but he argued no further since he was on the winning side. He rang for his secretary, and the new contract was dictated and signed.

Gordon and Royd went back to Nether Bolling, intent on continuing their work on optics before their precious threads of reasoning were lost in side issues.

But again there came interruption. That same after-noon, when they were ready to settle down to a long spell of work, Charles Irwin of the watch distributors telephoned.

"Dr. Royd, I must have thousands more watches!" he insisted. "They're selling very fast and I also have some export orders. Our financial returns for the month are tremendous. I'll send them to you in the morning along with our check and audit. Have you realized that if you can supply the demand you can become a millionaire?"

"Such a possibility had occurred to me," Royd admitted absently.

"What's the matter, doctor? Aren't you feeling well?"

"Oh, yes, thank you. Just preoccupied, that's all."

"Preoccupied? At a time like this! Dr. Royd, I don't think you understand what I'm saying. I want 20,000 watches as soon as you can deliver them."

"Very well, you shall have them," Royd promised. "And I'll look forward to your check for present sales. Now do forgive me. I'm in the midst of a vital experi-ment."

Royd put down the telephone and wandered back into the laboratory where Gordon was busily working. He glanced up briefly.

"Anything interesting from Irwin?" he asked, knowing from the maid's earlier announcement that who had been the caller.

"Apparently every watch has gone and he wants twenty thousand more as soon as possible."

"Good! We'll have to get that demand met— Look, Doc, it seems to me that if we electronized this wire with your special process we'd get the effect we're striving for. It would carry the light photons much more freely."

Royd nodded eagerly. "Yes, I believe it would. We must try it— Yes, Ellen?" he asked wearily, as the maid appeared in the doorway.

"This letter for Mr. Fryer, doctor. It just arrived."

Gordon took it, knowing immediately from whom it had come. Typewritten, express post, stamped east London. He tapped it against his thumbnail, and considered.

"Throw it away," Royd advised.

"I wish I were built that way," Gordon sighed, and tore the flap. There was a rather longer message this time:

> Thought I'd forgotten, didn't you, since I haven't reminded you for a month? Doing nicely with your watch and Spiritine, are you not? How much good are either going to be to you when October 19, 2019, comes round? You'll be surprised how quickly the time will go!

When Royd had read the card, Gordon tore it up savagely and flung it away. "So help me, Doc, I'll find Blessington before I'm finished and put a bullet through him!"

"And get yourself convicted of murder? Don't be an idiot!" Royd laid a hand on Gordon's arm. "Don't start thinking things like that, taking advantage of destiny. You'd be thrown in jail, and a man with a mind like yours is more useful to the community to wreck everything because of the venom of Blessington."

"I've got to take some kind of action!" Gordon snapped. He strode out of the laboratory and into the hall, spending some moments afterwards in browsing through the telephone directory. Finally he picked up the phone, ignoring the silent, watching figure of Royd in the laboratory.

"Hello! Climax Detective Agency? This is Gordon Fryer speaking— Yes, I'm that Gordon Fryer. I have a matter to put into your hands— Okay. Get me every detail you can concerning a man named Blessington, manufacturer of glass eyes somewhere in the east end of London. Whether he still manufactures glass eyes or has a place of business I don't know, but I want his address and every detail about him. He may even have changed his name— Oh, yes. Tall, hatchet-faced, and formerly a butler to Dr. Royd of the Larches, Nether Bolling. You may get some lead from the Employment Exchange. Send all the details to me at the Larches, Nether Bolling, Berkshire. Yes. Thanks."

Gordon put the phone down and met Royd's eyes across the hall.

"I mean it," Gordon said, his face grim. "And if I

can run Blessington into jail for causing me mental disquiet, I'm going to!"

* * * * * * *

But experienced though the sleuths of the Climax Detective Agency undoubtedly were, they failed to locate the elusive Blessington, and during the time they searched the Spring passed into Summer, and then into Autumn. By November, by which time five more cynical notes had been received, Gordon gave up the chase. The postal authorities refused to assist on the grounds that no law can stop anybody sending an express letter, and since they did not contain anything of a seditious nature the law could not operate.

The only solution did indeed seem to be to ignore the pinpricks, but this Gordon knew in his heart he could never do. There was an unholy fascination about the reminders, which he just could not thrust aside.

Mentally, he was less affected by them for his work on the synthetic eye, still only in its earliest stages, was all-absorbing. In other directions everything was working out perfectly. Spiritine was selling in greater quantities every day. It was really remarkable that Spiritine didn't sweep the market, but the public is notoriously suspicious of new fuels and always look for the catch in such inventions. Entire laboratories were now employed by Royd to turn out the liquid; and in the other direction the 'Forever Watch' was an accepted adornment on the wrists of most men and women.

By January of the following year Gordon knew that he could never want for money, but true to his word he insisted on Dr Royd having a fifty-fifty share—to which Royd retaliated by making Gordon accept fifty-fifty on Spiritine.

In February, Howard Crawford, the advance guard of the world's biggest petrol concern came to London, and after that to Nether Bolling and the Larches.

"I tell you plainly, gentlemen," the representative said, very neat and formal, "that you cannot go on selling your Spiritine."

Royd smiled and peered over his spectacles, but Gordon was plainly annoyed.

"You cannot dictate terms to us, Mr. Crawford! The Free Trade Act passed by Parliament recently gives us absolute liberty. If the public prefer our stuff to normal fuel, that is to our benefit."

"And our detriment," Crawford said. "When I said you cannot go on selling Spiritine, I meant that the petroleum companies, which I represent, cannot stand the competition. Equally, they cannot go out of business. So we must compromise."

"We cannot compromise for another eight weeks," Gordon said. "British Garages have us under contract."

"They'd break it for a consideration."

"In what amount?" Royd asked mildly.

Crawford reflected. "We are prepared to offer you fifteen million pounds for your formula, and we'll deal with all contracts into which you may have entered."

"This is a waste of time," Gordon said briefly.

"Twenty million, then."

"Try again when the contract runs out," Royd suggested.

"In eight more weeks Spiritine can make devastating inroads," Crawford snapped.

"We're still not interested," Gordon said flatly.

"Very well, gentlemen." Crawford tightened his lips. "Since that is your reaction, there is nothing more I can do at the moment. If you think further, here is the address of our temporary London headquarters. You'll find the city manager, Mr. Bayhurst, always ready to see you."

There were fixed smiles and bows, nothing more—then Royd and Gordon returned to the laboratory and looked at each other.

"What's the answer, Doc?" Gordon asked seriously. "It's your fuel, even though you insisted that I should take the credit for it. What do you want to do?"

"Let them climb to thirty million, then sell out. I don't want money, as such, but that formula is worth that sum—and more."

"And let the petrol companies handle the whole thing?"

"Why not? The distribution task is too vast for us to handle with so many other things preoccupying us. For the time being let's forget it."

To Royd at his age, with all the money he needed, this was no great effort, but it rankled in Gordon's mind that an obviously potential fuel empire should be so completely jettisoned. Still, the fuel was not strictly his, so he felt honor-bound to respect his old friend's wishes.

He worked until late March on his synthetic eye, having at last perfected a synthetic optic nerve of electronicized wire, before Royd referred to the Spiritine matter again—and then it was by way of a telegram that was delivered in the mid-morning of March 27.

"The shoe's pinching," Royd remarked. "Read for yourself."

Gordon looked at the telegram and smiled grimly. It said:

> Thirty million offered for immediate transfer of formula to ourselves. Respectfully urge you to consider this proposal. Bayhurst. World Petroleum.

"Well?" Gordon asked, raising his eyes.

"They can have it," Royd answered, quite decided. "Since it is supposed to be your fuel, in which I'm only a partner, you'd better go and settle the business. This eye work we're on can't be left, and—"

"It'll have to be for this, sir. Your signature as well as mine will be needed. Besides, I'm not handling this alone. It needs somebody with experience as well. I'll get out the car. We can be in London by afternoon."

They were, stopping half-an-hour for lunch at an hotel. By this time Gordon was quite resigned to trading in the formula for thirty million Sterling— then, when he and Royd had been whisked to the city manager's office in the lift, Gordon suddenly forgot all about the reason for his mission. His eyes were fixed on the woman who was evidently the manager's receptionist-secretary.

"Miss Haslam!" Gordon gasped, standing just inside the office doorway with Royd behind him.

"Eh?" Royd peered over his glasses. "Bless me, so it is!"

Virginia Haslarn rose from behind her desk and came forward. There was no smile on her face; only an expression of cold efficiency.

"Naturally," she said, "this will be a bigger surprise to you two gentlemen than it is to me. Since I phoned the telegram that Mr. Bayhurst gave me, I knew you'd be coming. He will see you right away—"

She turned, but Gordon's voice stopped her. "Just a moment, Miss Haslam. Let me get something straight. What are you doing here, working for World Petroleum?"

"I'm Mr. Bayhurst's secretary. Thanks to you, Mr. Fryer, I lost my job on the *Record*."

"Thanks to me! What did I do?"

"Killed my series about you. I finished up with a half-column, and a rival did half a page of guesswork. My boss just couldn't get over it, so I quit. My secretarial qualifications got me in here."

Gordon pinched finger and thumb into his eyes, trying to fathom the inscrutable drift of events which had brought the girl right back into his orbit again. If he had done as she had originally asked, she would not have been here now—

"Oh, what's the use!" he sighed, and she looked at him frigidly.

"I'll tell Mr. Bayhurst you're here," she said, and tapped on an adjoining door. As the gruff voice bade her enter, she glided out of sight—to presently reappear, pushing the door wide.

Gordon had one glimpse of her stony stare as he passed her, then with Royd beside him he was facing the city manager. He was thin-faced and gray-haired, and Gordon was sure that he had seen him before somewhere.

"Good of you to come, gentlemen." He shook hands vigorously, then waved them to a seat. "Cigars? Drinks?"

"Neither, thanks," Gordon answered. "We have very little time and would prefer to get on with the business."

"Simple enough. As you would gather from my telegram, we are prepared to offer you our check for thirty million pounds in return for the Spiritine formula. We have to admit that you've beaten us."

Gordon gave Royd a glance and the old scientist smiled.

"We are willing to accept the offer, Mr. Bayhurst, otherwise we wouldn't be here. Normally we would probably haggle over the amount, but with pressing experiments in various directions, we prefer to have Spiritine off our hands."

"Good! In that case we can settle the business right away." Bayhurst pressed the button on his desk and waited for Virginia Haslam to appear. "Oh, Miss Haslam, please bring me that contract I dictated this morning for Mr. Fryer, will you?"

"Yes, Mr. Bayhurst."

There was only a moment's interval and then she was back, the long folded document in her hand. There was a peculiar expression on her face as she reached the desk.

"You'd better stay," Bayhurst told her. "I shall need you as a witness."

She nodded, standing a little behind Gordon. He gave her a glance and then turned away. Unintentionally he found himself looking at the calendar—March 27, and it immediately brought into his mind the remembrance of a photograph—of Virginia restraining him, of a look of annoyance on the face of the man at the desk. For the first time Gordon resolved something: he realized why he recognized Bayhurst, although he had never met him before. Of course! The photograph for March 27!

"Do you wish to sign jointly, or is this matter entirely up to you, Mr. Fryer?" Bayhurst asked genially.

"Well, I—" Gordon began, then he was interrupted by a sudden outburst from Virginia.

"I've just got to speak!" she exclaimed, and Bayhurst stared at her blankly. "I can't let you do this, Mr. Fryer! Though our personal relations are not exactly cordial, I've too strong a sense of justice to allow you to sign away a colossal fortune. You mustn't! It isn't to be thought of!"

"Miss Haslam, if you please!" Bayhurst exploded.

"I'm sorry, Mr. Bayhurst." She swung on him, her color rising. "As your secretary I happen to know what you plan to make of Spiritine, and this thirty million for the formula is sheer daylight robbery with violence! There! Now I've said it and I may as well walk out and never come back. I'm not doing it because of you, Mr. Fryer, but because I don't like to see anybody snared and baited by a soulless combine."

She laid a hand on Gordon's arm, looking at him beseechingly, and Bayhurst glared.

"That's it," Gordon whispered, fascinated. "The very act, the very office, and you, Doc, just out of my sight there. It's happened! The Scanner's right again."

"Naturally," Royd said shrugging.

"What's the meaning of this?" Bayhurst roared, utterly at a loss: "Gentlemen, what are you talking about? Will you kindly sign and—"

"No!" Gordon rose to his feet. "I've had my doubts all along about the wisdom of this move, and now I'm sure. I needed the jolt Miss Haslam has given me. Sorry, Doc," he added, as he saw Royd looking at him over his spectacles.

"Nothing to be sorry about, my boy. But it will involve a tremendous amount of work getting things organized."

"I don't care if it does. If we look at it logically, Mr. Bayhurst must be prepared to make the whole of a lot more than thirty million if that's what he's prepared to give us."

"Multi-millions!" Virginia insisted breathlessly. "I know because I've seen the computations!"

"You're just the girl we want!" Gordon exclaimed, gripping her arm. "That is, if you can bear to talk to me."

She looked away almost shyly for a moment, then Bayhurst banged his desk.

"Gentlemen, where *are* we?" he demanded. "Surely you are not going to heed my secretary? She is simply—"

"Perfect," Gordon finished, grinning. "Sorry, Mr. Bayhurst, but she's completely reversed the situation. If anybody runs Spiritine, it'll be us."

With that he strode to the door and pulled it open, ushering the girl out before him. He and Royd waited long enough for her to gather her personal possessions and get into her hat and coat, then they took her with them to the nearest restaurant.

"Altogether, quite extraordinary," Royd commented, when the tea had been served.

"If I broke things up, I'm sorry," Virginia apologized. "I'm the kind of woman who speaks out—can't help it."

"Miss Haslam, consider yourself the chief secretary to the potential Spiritine Corporation," Gordon smiled. "And my profound apologies for the way I behaved when I first met you. I begin to see that one cannot defeat destiny."

"Destiny?" Virginia looked astonished.

"I'll explain more fully one day. For the moment

we'll be content with knowing what World Petroleum had planned to do with Spiritine."

"That will take time to explain. What I suggest is that I go to my rooms and work out in detail everything I can remember, and submit it to you. It should help tremendously."

"Good!" Gordon rubbed his hands together. "Tomorrow, then, we'll see you at the Larches and make the first moves to get Spiritine properly launched, using British Garages as our jumping off point."

"I hope," Royd remarked, "that you haven't forgotten our work on the synthetic eye, Gordon? We were going to abandon Spiritine so we wouldn't be held up with our experiments."

"I know—and we won't be. I have the feeling that Miss Haslam will take a tremendous weight off our shoulders."

Virginia gave a very direct look. "Mr. Fryer, don't start thinking that I'm a big executive, or anything. I certainly could not organize a Spiritine Corporation. The biggest thing I ever organized was a staff dance for the *Record*."

"That shows you have the talent, anyway." Gordon patted her hand. "Don't you worry. Something big's coming, and I have a particular reason for knowing it can't fail."

"What a lovely position to be in! How do you know?"

"As I said earlier, one day I'll tell you. Now let's get this tea finished, then we can drop you at your rooms on our way to Nether Bolling."

"In that case you'll have to take me the whole journey. I am still living in Nether Bolling and have traveled up here each day—and I must collect what salary I have due from Bayhurst, too."

* * * * * * *

That evening, when he had at last left Virginia in Nether Bolling—with her promise to turn up the following morning at the Larches with all the information she could recall—Gordon was a changed man. Certainly his mind was not on the synthetic eye, a fact that Royd was quick to notice.

"Gordon," he said seriously, "I've reached the age when romance doesn't mean a thing, but that doesn't imply that I expect you to feel the same. For all that, we have this job to do. You have a masterpiece here, and I'd never forgive myself if I allowed you to lose track of things because of a girl, no matter how desirable."

"I shan't lose track of things, Doc." Gordon lighted a cigarette and gazed absently before him. "This eye will succeed; otherwise, I wouldn't be standing before the B.O.A. in 2013."

"And how do you know you will receive praise? It might be censure!"

"Could be, though I have the feeling it won't."

"I thought," Royd continued, "that you had made up your mind to disprove the Scanner? Now I find you accepting its findings without reservations."

"What else can I do after what happened today?" Gordon said. "Just the same, I do not accept the inevitability of death in 2019! I'll find a way to circumvent that last incident. In the meantime I'm not struggling. I have too much regard for Virginia Haslam to do that."

"Then I suggest you try and forget Virginia Haslam for the moment and concentrate on this eye. There is a vast amount of work still to be done."

Gordon nodded and smiled sheepishly. Thereafter, for the rest of the evening, he and Royd kept at their task—and they were at work again early the following morning when Virginia arrived. They both downed tools for the time being, and spent most of the morning in the library studying the information the girl had gathered during her employment with World Petroleum.

"This shows you the ramifications which had been planned," she said. "In every country in the world. True, most of these relate to service stations owned by W.P., but the idea is there. There is no reason why we can't get every non-combine service station to work with us and for us."

"We can, and we shall," Gordon decided. "British Garages can give Spiritine the initial send-off, then we'll stem out from that."

So, from such an inconspicuous beginning the potential Spiritine Corporation took root, and Virginia herself, possessed of a surprisingly keen business acumen, did most of the arranging and planning once she realized the nature of the experiment which was keeping Gordon and Royd so busy.

* * * * * * *

By late May, British Garages, now under a new contract, had extended Spiritine to every one of their organizations at home and abroad. By the end of August other garages were selling out their contracts that bound them to World Gasoline and seeking to install Spiritine instead. The new fluid was taking the place of petroleum. Aviation was the last group to become interested, and when they did Spiritine was ordered as the sole fuel for all aircraft.

How much of this rolling tide of prosperity was due to her own efforts only Virginia Haslam knew. She it was who made arrangements, after consultation with Dr. Royd, for the necessary laboratories to be contracted for the manufacture of the fuel. She it was who approved the plans for the building in London which was the new headquarters of the Spiritine Corporation, she herself being one of the directors and, indeed, the chief voice behind every move the corporation made.

By January of the following year Spiritine was definitely established, and the drift of wealth and power forced Gordon out of his secluded position as companion to Dr. Royd. He was compelled to take an active interest in the Corporation's affairs and devote what spare time he could to the synthetic eye, still a long way from being perfected.

Dr. Royd had accepted the inevitable in losing Gordon as his constant companion, but the break was not absolute, for at every opportunity Gordon presented himself and added a little more to the perfection of the synthetic eye. It was usually at these times that he found one of the Blessington notes awaiting him—and he always read them, but so immense was the current of success around him the pinpricks did not hurt nearly as much as they had once.

In the June of 2008 Gordon abandoned his London apartment and began looking for a residence compatible with his wealth—and inevitably Virginia Haslam accompanied him, though as far as she knew it was in a strictly business capacity. The only thing she could not understand was Gordon's complete indifference to every dwelling she discovered until at length one had seemed to take his fancy and he insisted on driving out to see it. It lay near Reading and therefore was conveniently halfway between Nether Bolling and London.

"There is a lot about you that still puzzles me, Gordon," Virginia said, as they drove down the summery country lanes. "I've known you for quite a time now, and have seen you in every mood. I've discovered you're a scientific genius with a not very well developed business sense. But back of all that there is a cloudy something, and I just can't put my finger on it."

"Would it matter if you did?" he asked.

She glanced at him. Though he was still only in the late twenties and tremendously active physically and mentally, there were signs of corpulence developing, and already his hair was graying over the ears.

"It would," she answered. "I haven't worked beside you for so long, and respected your abilities without it doing something to me. I want to—to help you."

"Help me?" Gordon laughed incredulously. "That's a good one! I've made, and probably shall continue to make, millions from a wonder-watch and a wonder-fuel. I've perfect health, and yet you want to help me! To do what?"

"Find yourself."

Gordon stopped the car. Just here city life might have been just a dream. There were only the rolling green fields, verdant hedges, and a blue sky looking as though a careless painter had smeared a white brush over parts of it.

"Find myself," Gordon repeated, musing.

"You've never behaved like yourself from the moment I met you," Virginia continued. "I never really believed you when you blew up in the café that day and told me to keep out of your life. You're always trying to avoid something, and if for some reason you don't wish to tell me what it is, then at least let me try to help you escape it."

"You can't help me, Virgie." Gordon studied her earnest eyes and the wind-swept blonde hair. "Not a soul in the world can help me. You see, I—I know when I am going to die."

Her expression changed. "Die! You mean there's something wrong with you? That doctors—"

"Doctors, nothing! Never saw one in my life. No, it's a matter of science. I've had dealings with a machine, which has shown me the exact date of my death. I wish to heaven I'd never discovered that date. Night and day I cannot escape it. It's become a part of me. Even when other things crowd into my mind, I can never escape that one date with destiny."

"Will it be—soon?"

"Soon enough. I'll be thirty-eight, October nineteenth, 2019."

For a long time Virgie gazed out over the fields, then without looking at Gordon she said:

"Why frighten yourself? You can't possibly be sure! What kind of a machine was it? One of those fairground things?"

"It was an invention of the cleverest scientist I've ever known—our mutual friend, Dr. Royd. I saw, in photographic form, six incidents out of my future life. Up to now every one has come true, in spite of my efforts to sidestep the issue. That being so, I'm haunted by the fact that the remainder will come true also—including the last one."

"Now I think I understand! Was it because of something you had seen in these photographs that you behaved so oddly the first time I met you?"

"It was. I knew also that I would meet you in the office of the gasoline company, but I didn't know it was theirs at the time, of course. To evade that, I tried to push you out of my life, but you sprang back again and, once more, everything happened to schedule."

"I see," the girl said finally. "And what else did you see besides my advent and your death?"

"Success, probably, with the synthetic eye I'm working on and...." Gordon stopped.

"Well?"

Gordon moved slightly and looked at her. "I saw what appeared to be our marriage."

"Which is one thing you can make come true—or not," the girl said deliberately. "You can refuse to ask me to marry you, or I can reject you when you do ask. That way the spell will be broken."

"There are some things stronger than spells, Virgie—and human love is one of them. Machines, destiny, or anything else, I want you to marry me. If you want to break the schedule, you can refuse."

"And who am I to let a schedule interfere with the one thing I've wanted ever since I first met you? I'll marry you, Gordon, gladly—and that will mean you'll have me on your side to disprove this terror that has come into our lives."

Gordon smiled and kissed her gently. It was an hour before he drove the car on again and they stopped in Reading for lunch. Then towards half-past two they reached the house they were seeking. That it was the right one he knew only too well: the photograph of future time was proof of that.

"By rights," he said, "we should refuse to take this place and again try and break the schedule. I knew it was the one when the estate agent gave us the view of it. What do you suggest we do about it? Find another?"

The girl shook her head. "No. That would be running away from a threat, and you never defeat a threat that way. We'll take it. The one thing we really do need to sidestep, it seems, are the circumstances which lead up to the final scene you saw—and that we will do together."

Gordon hugged her gently. "Let's look the place over. We don't even know that it will be satisfactory.

But it was, as he inwardly knew it would be. And the place was reasonably priced—so there just did not seem to be any logical reason for turning it down.

Nor did he. When he and Virginia arrived back in London in the late afternoon, they were just in time to catch the estate agent in, and the bank transfer and conveyance of property was completed. And Gordon still wondered. Had he done right, or wrong, in thus bowing to the dictates of destiny?

* * * * * * *

Royd, for his part, when he heard the news of the engagement, took it with his mature calmness—but his congratulations were sincere. And, when Gordon and Virginia were married a month later, his wedding gift consisted of a cot and nursery furnishings, together with equipment for a baby's every need. Whether or not he caused embarrassment to the two young people Royd did not know: he merely viewed the matter with scientific detachment, knowing—as Gordon did— from photographs the inevitable result of the union.

It did not improve Gordon's temper to receive, when he and Virginia were enjoying their honeymoon in Cannes, a registered letter from east London, containing the customary square card.

Virginia read it also, and here in the brilliant sunshine and in the midst of the greatest bliss of their lives the words seemed to have a queer, other-world quality:

> Wherever you go you cannot escape me, or
> Destiny. I know your every move, even though
> it costs me a fair amount to keep track of you.
> What do you hope to gain from this marriage
> when you have only twelve more years to live?
> One year of the thirteen has gone: how much
> more quickly the others will go!

"Just what kind of a man is this Blessington?"
Virgmia asked, puzzled, when she had read the note
through. "You've given me odd hints, but what was he
like to know?"

"Cold, hard, cynical. All this has happened because
I queered his comfortable pitch in Dr. Royd's home."

"I find it hard to believe that anybody, no matter how
vindictive, would stay bitter so long!"

"Blessington would," Gordon answered with conviction. "It only costs him a stamp—and the wages of
whoever he has watching my moves—and I suppose
he thinks that repays him. He knows the stab I must
get when these things arrive."

"He doesn't know you read them, though?"

"True, but he'll know that the very sight of the envelope must be enough. Time and again I've vowed to
find him and have the issue out with him, but I can't
trace him."

"Nobody is that hard to find, surely. Who have you
had looking for him?"

"Climax Detective Agency, about a year ago. Cost

me a mint and I got nowhere."

"With the position you have these days, there's nothing to prevent you telling Scotland Yard. Have the nuisance stopped."

Gordon reflected, then he gave a resolute nod. "I'll do that right now! Be back in a moment—" He departed from the hotel terrace for the nearest telephone and was absent nearly fifteen minutes. When he returned he was smiling. "Light of my life, you hit the nail on the head! The thought that Gordon Fryer, the great inventor of Spiritine and co-inventor of the 'Forever Watch', should be the victim of disquieting notes is too much for one Chief-Inspector Bland, and he's going to look into the matter—or his men are! Now let's forget all about the beastly business and go for a swim."

* * * * * * *

The return to London was made a month later, and thence they traveled to their home in Higher Newton. When, the next day, they visited Royd, they discovered that the latest returns on Spiritine and the wonder watch were in—with no let-up in the sales of either product.

"In fact, Doc, we're rich, eh?" Gordon grinned.

"Obviously, my boy! And did you two young people have a happy honeymoon?"

They looked at each other and smiled; then almost immediately Royd switched back to business.

"I'm glad you've returned, Gordon, not only because of meetings to be attended on behalf of Spiritine and the watch, but also because I've got the last links in this eye business. I want your opinion."

"You mean you've finished it?" Gordon asked in surprise.

"I think so. Take a look at it."

Gordon moved to the bench where the synthetic eye lay on a velvet square. In every possible way it duplicated a normal eye, except that its interior was composed of wires, fluids, and minute lenses, all terminating in a long, hair-thick electronicized wire trailing from the back of the eye.

"It will turn on these rotor bearings which take the place of muscles," Royd explained, indicating the swiveling system. "I think that Blessington with his glass eye must have used something similar, but the eye you found hadn't been developed to that extent. Anatomically, I have duplicated everything needful, so the rest is up to Sir Hartley."

"Whom?" Gordon asked, glancing up.

"Sir Hartley Farrow, about the best eye surgeon in London. I asked him to come over later today and see what he thinks of this idea, and whether a surgical linking-up is feasible."

"The whole conception seems to me to be particularly marvelous," Virginia said. "Outside the boon it will be to Mankind in general, if it works you'll go down in history, Dr. Royd."

"You mean Gordon will," Royd smiled, "He had the right idea even when I couldn't see anything in it. All I have done is improve on his ideas."

"I think you're overdoing the modesty, sir," Gordon said. "Whatever comes of this, it's 50-50, as usual."

"As you wish, Gordon, but—yes, Ellen?" Royd looked up as the maid appeared.

"There's an Inspector Bland here, Mr. Fryer, to see you. He couldn't get you at your home."

"Bland!" Gordon's face brightened. "Show him in here, Ellen, please."

When the maid had gone Royd gave a curious glance. "What's all this about, Gordon? Been doing something you couldn't?"

"Not a bit. This concerns Blessington."

In a few moments Chief-Inspector Bland was shown in—tall, broad-shouldered, and quietly dressed. He briefly displayed his warrant-card and then shook hands.

"Nobody at your home, Mr. Fryer," he explained, "but I gathered from your recent letter that you'd be back by now, so I rang up here and the maid told me the rest— Now, do you wish to have a little private chat, or—"

"No, no, we can talk here. Have a chair, Inspector— Now, have you traced that swine Blessington?"

"We have sir, yes. Took a bit of doing, too. Blessington is trading under the name of the Zenith Glass Eye Manufacturers, and he had a medium-sized factory and headquarters in the London Docks area. He's calling himself Barton, but there's no doubt but what he's Blessington. So far we haven't pinned anything on him because that's really up to you. What's the charge to be?"

"Technically I don't know. He has sent me dozens of letters calculated to cause me a good deal of mental anguish. Incidentally, I'm assuming that Blessington is the culprit. I've no proof it is Blessington who's sent me the notes."

"We have that proof, sir," Brand said. "We've traced the post office from which the letters were sent and the person sending them. The description is exact. All right, we'll fix the charge and see that he's summoned. I'd suggest you put the whole thing in the hands of your lawyer and leave it at that."

"I will," Gordon promised. "And thanks for finding him. I want him to be taught the most savage lesson the law can devise. Destroying peace of mind is worse than murder, in my destination."

Bland rose, shook hands, and took his departure. Gordon gave a sigh of relief when the door had closed.

"If this doesn't make Blessington sit up, nothing will," he said.

"Do you still intend to put a bullet through him?" Royd asked rather dryly.

"I don't quite know." Gordon mused for a moment. "The wish to do so is there, but—I'll think it over."

CHAPTER FIVE

THE FRYER EYE

Not long after the Inspector left, Sir Hartley Farrow arrived.

"I must apologize for coming earlier than I had intended," the ophthalmic surgeon said, "but I have an important appointment later today, so I just crammed this visit in. What's it all about, Dr. Royd? New sort of glass eye, didn't you say?"

Royd motioned to chairs and all four seated themselves.

"I said a synthetic eye," Royd corrected, "which is a vastly different thing. Credit for the invention belongs to Mr. Fryer here. I have added certain modifications."

The surgeon smiled. "In fact, quite a combination of genius! The famous Dr. Royd, and the equally famous creator of our newest fuel. Believe me, it was only the combination of your two names that made me come so far out of my way to see you."

"Here it is," Royd said, picking up the eye. "An exact duplicate of the human eye, with the one enormous advantage that it can see—or should. That is the one point on which we are not sure. Which is where you come in. What is your opinion?"

Sir Hartley picked up the eye and pondered it carefully.

"Beautifully intricate," he said. "The cleverest piece of mechanism I've yet seen—insofar as duplicating an organ of the human body is concerned. As to whether it will fulfill your hopes, I don't know. I cannot know without trying it."

"Which is exactly what we want you to do," Gordon said.

"Yes, I'm aware of that, but you two gentlemen in your scientific endeavor seem to have overlooked something. I cannot, by law, use this device. Ethics forbid it. I don't doubt that legislation could be passed making it legal to adopt such an eye, but to get that legislation we need proof that the eye will work. So you see, it's a vicious circle."

Gordon stared blankly. "You mean to tell me that we have a boon to give to humanity and can't use it without all that palaver?"

The surgeon shrugged. "The law's an ass, Mr. Fryer. That's an old saying."

"Can't you even try it on somebody who'd be willing to experiment?" Virginia prompted.

"No. Or if I did, I'd risk my professional reputation."

Then Royd said: "Is there any law preventing you using it on an animal?"

"No. Animals are the poor victims until we reach the human stage. But unfortunately, the anatomy of an animal is so different from that of a human I couldn't attempt it. I'm not a veterinary surgeon, remember."

"How about an ape, or a monkey, which most nearly resembles a human?" Gordon asked. "I'd buy one from the zoo if you could use it."

Sir Hartley considered for a long moment, then with a shake of his head put the eye back on its velvet square. "No. Mr. Fryer, I wouldn't attempt it. Even the ape or monkey has cranial differences to the human, which could make the link-up most complicated and difficult. The only way is to find some non-human method of proving that this eye works, and then get the necessary legislation."

"In your view," Gordon asked, "can you see any reason why this eye should not work in the way that we think?"

"I believe it would work, yes—but it is only my private opinion, not to be quotred publicly."

Gordon reflected. "Since you cannot accept a volunteer, Sir Hartley, without perhaps endangering your reputation, it is no use my offering myself—and I have enough faith in the eye to do so. The only other alternative is for me to convince the British Optical Association that a test operation should be performed. They, I take it, are the ones you are bothered about?"

"That's so. If they give permission, then I'll do anything you wish. Otherwise—no."

With that the surgeon took his departure with the promise that he would act the moment he was free to do so.

"Which settles it," Gordon said resolutely, carefully

wrapping the eye in its velvet square and then transferring it to a metal box. "I'm going this very moment to the BOA, Doc., and I shan't return until I get their permission. Everything depends on it. Care to come with me?"

"I'd like to, but I think it would be better if I stayed away. I want you to have all the credit for this idea, Gordon. Besides, I have reached a crisis in my diatomic experiment and don't wish to leave it."

Gordon nodded. "Okay. Virgie and I will go."

They drove to central London, saw the president of the BOA, and Gordon explained the eye.

"If all you say is true," the president said, "you are offering an invention which will banish blindness from the face of the earth. How immeasurably great such a boon would be is obvious. I'll see what I can do, Mr. Fryer, about calling a meeting and ring your home the moment a decision is reached."

"You wish me to leave the eye with you?"

"If you will. It will make it easier for me to explain to my associates."

Arriving back in Nether Bolling, they informed Royd, at work on his diatoms, of their progress and then returned home.

On the following day London appointments with their various business interests kept Gordon, Virginia, and Royd busy. They returned to Nether Bolling— and Royd's home—to find a phone message had been left by Chief-Inspector Bland. It stated briefly that a summons had been issued against Blessington and further developments would be soon forthcoming.

This fact sent Gordon to his London lawyer the day afterwards.

He came back home to learn from a gladsome Virginia that the President of the BOA had phoned in the interval, announcing that he had managed to convince his associates it was worth their while to permit an experimental operation to test the synthetic eye.

Thereafter Gordon found himself the center of two exciting events—the one the case against Blessington, which ended with him getting a sentence of twelve years' imprisonment, chiefly because it came to light during the trial that he had indulged in systematic robbery of scientific equipment whilst in Royd's employ, and of which fact the absent-minded Royd had not been aware until he had come to check up—and also because his notes to Gordon were proven by the prosecution to amount to extreme mental cruelty and not far short of mental murder.

The second exciting event for Gordon was the information from Sir Hartley Farrow that a case had come under his observation wherein the experimental operation might be performed. It would be some days before he could make an announcement.

"Y'know," Gordon remarked, when he was driving back home again to Nether Bolling at the conclusion of the Blessington affair, "it's an odd thought, but Blessington will live again in twelve years, or less with remission, and I'll die. Funny the way things work out!"

"They haven't yet," Virginia said sharply. "Gordon, for heaven's sake stop harping on the wrong side! You're only making things tougher to overcome."

"Sorry. Just can't help getting into that mood sometimes."

"I suppose his business will just collapse?" Virginia mused.

"Who cares?" Gordon snapped.

Which as far as he was concerned, killed the matter. From that moment his attention was given to the synthetic eyes experiment, and in the ensuing days his impatience became almost intolerable, both to himself and Virginia. It was one of those periods when the watch and Spiritine concerns did not need any attention, and he was not actively engaged on anything scientific with Dr. Royd—so all he could do was wait, and fret—and wait.

Then came news, on an early September morning. Sir Hartley himself was on the wire.

"You've done it, Fryer!" came his enthusiastic voice. "Sorry to have kept you so long, but I had to wait until Nature adjusted the balance for my patient. He was operated on after an explosion in a chemical factory, which destroyed his right eye. I replaced it with the synthetic eye, and he tells me he can see perfectly with it—even better than with his former eye, the reason being, of course, that the synthetic one is not subject to the deterioration of the flesh and blood organism."

"Marvelous!" Gordon exclaimed, his face bright. "And it couldn't have been done without you to link things up. What's the next move?"

"I shall report the whole case to the BOA and take my patient with me as proof. There's no doubt about what you have inaugurated a new era for humanity, Fryer, and destroyed one of its greatest curses. My recommendation is that colleges be opened immediately for the training of surgeons under my direction so they can follow my methods of link-up. As for you, the way is obvious. Tens of thousands of synthetic eyes are needed. We can conquer everything from total blindness to common astigmatism. Perhaps you'd better come to London and explain everything to the BOA."

"I haven't the time," Gordon responded. "It will take me every moment to get those eyes ready. I'll make a specimen and then select the correct laboratories for their manufacture."

"As to the financial side, you are going to make another fortune," Sir Hartley remarked dryly. "What a gift you have in that direction, Fryer!"

"I don't want a cent," Gordon replied. "I'm giving this boon to humanity free of cost, as far as I'm concerned. How the Government will react is nothing to do with me. I'm no religionist, but I have the feeling that that great idea was given directly to me for the benefit of everybody, and I don't want paying for it."

"For which the world will eternally bless you," the surgeon said quietly. "I shall insist that the BOA name this miracle the 'Fryer Eye'. Now I must get busy. Keep in touch and let me know what develops."

Gordon rang off and swung to find Virginia smiling

at him. He caught at her shoulders, searching her face.

"You heard, Virgie?"

"Yes, every word. You've laid another stone in the edifice of human achievement."

"To me," Gordon said, "there is something about this eye business which lifts me right out of the rut of ordinary commercialism. The watch and the wonder-fuel are useful, and have made and are still making vast amounts of money—but this is really something! Now I know how Lister and Pasteur must have felt."

Virginia patted his arm. "I know just how you feel, Gordon. You know I do."

"I could probably do other things, if I had the time." His brows knitted. "That's the screaming injustice of it all, Virgie! Here am I, gifted with an unusual scientific bent, yet cursed with only the waning years in which to use it. What could I not do with a life span like Royd knows he has! Ninety-three! Why, by that time I could—"

Gordon stopped, realizing the girl's hazel eyes were upon him. They were not exactly accusing, but—

"We agreed to forget it, or plan against it—but never to admit it," she reminded him. "Now you'd better let Dr. Royd know what has happened, hadn't you?"

"We'll drive over right away. This is far too good to send over the phone. Slip your things on."

Virginia nodded and hurried from the room. Gordon joined her at the car, where the chauffeur was waiting, and within half an hour they were in Royd's laboratory. As usual, he was pottering around in his untidy overalls, but on this occasion there was a curious, suppressed gleam in his eyes.

"So there we are," Gordon finished, when he had related the conversation with Sir Hartley. "I'm right on top of the world at the moment, Doc— However, something just occurs to me. Maybe I was a bit hasty in saying I'd give the Eye to humanity with my blessing. I'd overlooked the fact that I said we'd split fifty-fifty on whatever accrued."

"We can still do that," Royd smiled. "Fifty percent of nothing is nothing. Forget it, son. I'd sooner have the thanks of a suffering world than all the money there is. You did rightly."

Gordon began to move actively. "We've a lot to do, Doc. A specimen eye to make, laboratories to contact, distribution to arrange."

"Surely, surely. We'll manage it, with Virgie's help. I don't know what we'd do without her. She can arrange for the laboratories and distribution whilst you and I make the specimen eye. Now, whilst you're here, I have something else pretty marvelous to tell you. I was going to ring you up, but your arrival forestalled me."

"The only thing I would now consider as marvelous," Gordon said, "would be to learn that your Scanner sideslipped when it read the later stages of my brain."

"No, Gordon, it didn't slip up, but I believe I have discovered something which ought to make you, and lots of other people—if they want it—live to be two hundred years old!"

Gordon exchanged a blank look with Virginia.

"Diatoms," Royd explained, motioning to them in the enormous transparent bowl. "You recall that my idea was to test their cellular reaction to the particular fluid in which they were living? Well, I've found a fluid there which has increased the resistive energy of the diatoms by at least six times."

"Interpreted, what does that mean?" Virginia asked. "Can humans get the same way?"

"They can, by the extremely simple process of drinking the fluid. It will pass into the bloodstream, which will automatically feed the entire system. The result of that will be that the cells will decay less rapidly, building up the whole body into an extremely resistant state."

"More plainly, the elixir of Life?" Virginia suggested.

"In a way, yes, but it does not make one immortal. One can only have life prolonged. Look, let me show you what I mean."

Royd motioned and Gordon and Virginia followed him out of the laboratory into the adjoining department where he kept livestock, chiefly for experimental purposes. From its pen he released a piglet, caught it, and then held it with a practiced hand.

"Give me that knife," he instructed Gordon, nodding towards the bench.

Though he looked startled, Gordon did as he was told. Royd took it with his free hand and then deliberately ran the tip of the razor-keen blade down the squealing piglet's back. Virginia gave a little gasp of horror and Gordon turned away sharply—but their fears were not realized. The piglet was not in the least hurt. There was not even a line showing on the pink skin.

"You see?" Royd asked smiling, as he maneuvered the animal back into its pen. "Its cells have become so hardened with my Tensile-X, as I call it, that they do not break even under the direct cut of a knife. Nor is the toughness limited to the outer skin. It exists in every cell, in every organ. I have made the most exhaustive tests in order to be sure. As yet I haven't tried it on any human being, but I hope to soon."

His eyes rested on Gordon and Gordon gave a shrug.

"No use looking at me, Doc. I'm booked at thirty-eight according to the Scanner, and if your statements are to be believed, I can't sidestep it by using a wonder fluid. I'd suggest that *you* try it. It may account for the fact that you will live to be ninety-three. Quite frankly, from your build and general appearance, I can't see you doing it in the ordinary way."

"Certainly I shall try it because I have every faith in it," Royd replied. "But I may as well tell you that I devised it in the first place for your sake—an effort to try and defeat the fate which is apparently to over-take you. It seems likely that a railway accident brings about the end. With your body and cells hardened by this Tensile-X, only a direct injury to the heart could possibly kill you. Ordinary wounds just couldn't happen—as witness the piglet."

Gordon smiled dubiously. "Now you're reversing your own declaration, Doc! You have said all along that nothing can defeat Destiny, yet here you are offering Tensile-X as a means by which to do it. It doesn't make sense!"

"In my heart, and as a logician, I do not dare to believe that a forecast of future time can be incorrect, because if I do it tears up the whole fabric of mathematics and invariable law. On the other hand, as a human man, I could have made an error somewhere, either in the Scanner itself, or in my reasoning, and because of that I am willing to make an effort to try and cheat death. Why not try Tensile-X and see what happens? If it doesn't do any good, it certainly can't do any harm."

"Okay, I'll risk it," Gordon assented, after Virginia had given a confirmatory nod. "But it won't be the stuff out of that bowl of diatoms, surely?"

Royd laughed. "Good heavens, no! I have it specially prepared in bottles. I'll try some—and you too, Virgie, if you wish."

"What have I got to lose?" she responded. "If the miracle comes off, I don't want to become a doddering old wreck whilst Gordon sails on to a cheerful two hundred or something. Certainly I'll try some."

Royd nodded and led the way back into the laboratory; then he said: "Should this stuff prove correct, and in about a week we find that experiments with knives and bullets have no effect upon us, I'll set about interesting the medical world. This coming on top of the Eye should give us an immediate hearing."

Crossing to a cupboard he took from it a tightly

corked glass vial in which reposed a fluid of deep amber, similar to that in which the curious diatoms and clouds of algae were floating. With a certain solemnity he poured the fluid into three whisky-sized glasses and handed it over.

"Sure it won't poison us?" Virgie asked uneasily.

"Certain," Gordon answered for her. "Don't forget, I've seen a picture of us together in 2010, so we shan't be underground! Here goes, and may it be the foundation of yet another mighty achievement."

He drank the fluid at a gulp. It was oily and sweet, rather like glycerine, but if he anticipated any immediate result he was disappointed. In silence he watched Royd and Virginia drink off theirs.

"You will never realize you have taken it," Royd said, putting the glasses in the sink. "Its action on the cells will take place unnoticed, but don't start any experiments with knives until I give you the word."

There was silence for a moment, then Gordon clapped his hands together emphatically. "Well, that's that! Now how about getting that Eye under way, Doc, whilst Virgie makes the preliminary arrangements for its manufacture and distribution?"

* * * * * * *

So exacting were the details of the Eye, and so long the periods they worked at it, Gordon and Royd forgot all about the Tensile-X which was at work on them. Now and again Virginia thought of it, but even in her case the demands of organization for the Eye absorbed her so completely she had no time for anything else.

Then, at the close of a hectic fortnight—during which time there had been many urgent demands for speed from Sir Hartley Farrow—the task was complete and the pattern-Eye finished. Immediately it was rushed off to the major laboratory, from which other laboratories would take their models.

"Which," Gordon said, as he and Virgie spent the evening at home for the first time in two weeks, "about finishes the matter as far as we are concerned. The Government or the BOA will take things over from here."

He smiled as he sprawled in a big armchair in the twilight. "It's quite an extraordinary feeling," he added, "but at the moment there isn't anything claiming our immediate attention. Spiritine and the watch are running on oiled wheels with reliable staffs to handle them, so maybe it's about time I busied myself with seeing what I can do next."

"There's one thing," Virginia said, and getting up from her chair she crossed to the sideboard, returning with a sharp, pearl-handled carving knife.

"What the—?" Gordon looked at her blankly.

"Probably you've forgotten. I nearly had myself. By this time we ought to be as tough as leather if Dr. Royd's Tensile-X is working."

Gordon started. "So we should! He said a week, and a fortnight has gone by—but he also said we should consult him first."

"Easy enough. The phone's at your elbow."

Gordon raised it from its rest, ringing Royd's number. In a moment or two the scientist answered.

"Hello, Doc! Gordon here. What about this Tensile-X experiment? Virgie has just remembered it. Is it safe to see if anything happens from a knife wound?"

"Quite safe, yes. I just tried it out myself, with most gratifying results. Let me know how you two go on."

"Right. 'Bye for now." Gordon put the phone down again and then took the knife the girl held out to him. For some moments he played about with it, then summoning up his courage he drew the sharp point across the palm of his hand. Though he distinctly felt the thin edge of the blade it was as if he were using the back of it. A fast dissolving white line was all that showed as the result of his efforts.

"I believe it's right," he exclaimed blankly. "Here— you try. You should be more sensitive, as a woman."

Virgie tried, using the outside of her bare forearm, but the blade made no effect. Suddenly resolute, Gordon hurried from the lounge and returned with a safety-razor blade.

"This," he said grimly, "is really the acid test. The blade is a new one."

New or otherwise it made no impression, either on himself or Virgie. Finally he set the blade aside and stood musing whilst the girl sank back into her armchair.

"According to this," Gordon said at last, his voice still incredulous, "we ought to live until we're two hundred, and yet as far as I am concerned the Scanner said—" to came to an abrupt stop, lost in thought. He was silent for such a long time that Virgie looked up in enquiry.

"Anything wrong, Gordon? From my point of view it looks to me as if you have been given a fighting chance. In this tough condition, if it lasts—and there's no reason why it should not—you can't possibly get damaged in that railway accident. Remember what Dr. Royd said—only direct damage to the heart can kill."

"Uh-huh." Gordon gazed out into the twilight absently. It seemed he was about to say something, then he swung as the phone rang. Picking it up, he discovered Royd at the other end of the wire.

"Tried it out, Gordon?"

"Yes. It's all you claim for it. Knives won't touch us."

"Neither will bullets, if you care to try them. I have, but they fly back as though they had hit iron-hard rubber. Near as I can tell," Royd's thoughtful voice continued, "this stuff reacts much more potently on the human system than on the animal. A bullet will penetrate my experimental piglet—as the poor creature has discovered—but it won't penetrate me. Possibly the cellular build-up is much thicker in the case of human beings."

"You did say the heart was vulnerable," Gordon pointed out. "That still goes, doesn't it?"

"I'm afraid it doesn't. The area around the heart is very thickly protected and, from my own experiments, I find no penetration is possible."

"You mean," Gordon asked blankly, "that you actually tried shooting yourself through the heart?"

"Yes. Since I am not supposed to die until ninety-three, I risked it. I proved my point. I have no impression of where the bullet struck, and the same thing will apply to you and Virgie, probably more so since you are younger."

"Oh!" Gordon said, somewhat dully. "I'll—I'll ring you later, Doc, when we've weighed things up. This business takes a devil of a lot of assimilating."

He rang off and then sat looking at Virgie's enquiring face in the firelight. Finally he got up switched on the standard lamp, and came back to where the girl was seated.

"Apparently," he said, "the Doc has made us immortal," and he gave the details of the conversation he had had.

The girl leapt up, her eyes bright. "Then why so dull, Gordon? This is the very thing we've been hoping for! You can't possibly die at thirty-eight now! There's a mistake somewhere! We can be together for—for a century maybe or even longer. Perhaps, in time, the stuff might even make us immortal. Not only us either, but everybody."

Gordon ran a hand through his hair. "Frankly. Virgie, I just don't know what to think! As for us being immortal—well, we'd probably be sick of each other long before that. And I still can't see why this mysterious change has come into things, because if the Scanner is to be believed—" He sighed and shook his head. "No, I don't get it. The only thing I do know is that my last weapon has been taken from me and I've only just realized it."

"What weapon?"

"I had resolved, if things got too tough for me towards the finish, that rather than wait for the fatal date and be dragged helplessly into a series of experiences which would inevitably lead me to death, I'd kill myself. Get it all over cleanly. Cowardly, I know, but it was in my mind. That is, if it were possible. This infernal law of Time might somehow prevent it."

Virginia only smiled. "One way or another, para-doxes notwithstanding, we'll be together on this mortal coil for a long time yet. Do try and believe that!"

Gordon nodded, but it was plain his thoughts were pretty chaotic, as indeed they were. He was definitely a man who did not know what to believe—so it was probably a blessing that as the months began to slip by, work of various kinds kept him fully occupied, prin-cipally because Virginia had to retire from her usual activities with the approach of a blessed event.

Royd, for his part, handed on his Tensile-X to the Medical Association, who would indeed have passed it for public use—but the Government stepped in. Already Britain was overcrowded, and the possibility of extending life indefinitely was not looked upon as a favorable prospect. Countries less thickly populated might beneficially use the 'potion', but if they were allowed to and not Britain an ugly situation might arise—so Tensile-X was rejected, leaving only three people who had ever partaken of the stuff.

Apparently, it made no difference to the general level of health. Royd, Gordon, and Virgie were in neither better nor worse health than formerly, but they did find that the fluid seemed to reach its maximum efficiency within the first month, after which no further hardening seemed to take place.

Then some time after the drug had been rejected, there came an echo of it in May of the following year, 2008, just after Virginia's daughter had been born, and it came in the form of a summons from the Medical Association sent direct to Dr. Royd.

Puzzled by the apparent urgency of the letter, he visited the Medical headquarters in London, and found himself in the midst of an interview with Sir Basil Remlatt, president of the Association.

"I felt I should send for you, Dr. Royd, as the creator of Tensile-X," he explained, coming right to the point. "You submitted your formula and a sample, and both have of course been treated in the strictest confidence. However, certain of our analysts have been making further tests to see if there is anything which can be done by which we can get around the rather unreasonable Government attitude. In the course of these tests, something rather alarming has come to light."

"Alarming?" Royd repeated in surprise. "I don't see how that could be. I made every possible allowance—"

"Except the one of time, doctor. You couldn't allow for that, because only time itself could show."

"Neither could you, so what have you discovered?"

"Theoretically," the president said, "we believe that

Tensile-X, after a period of about ten years, will lose its power over bone structure, though not over cellular. That ingredient of napthadrine which you have used will create slow bone deterioration, leaving the person concerned—had anybody ever used the stuff—with a leathery-strong fleshly covering and a skeleton structure as brittle as glass. Not a pleasant prospect, Dr. Royd."

"At the best a theory," Royd commented.

"Rather more, perhaps. Our analysts have tested the stuff on white mice and, after a month, one of the mice was killed and examined. The dim beginnings of bone disintegration were already showing. It is a simple matter to calculate, from a given point of decay, how long it will take for the entire mass to collapse. Hence the estimate of ten years."

Royd was silent for a few moments, apparently not in the least disturbed. Being a true scientist, he viewed the matter with complete impartiality.

"Which," he observed finally, "definitely rules out Tensile-X as a public proposition."

"Definitely! Unless you can think up something that rids the drug of this dangerous corrosive effect. I thought you ought to know how things stand."

Royd smiled and rose to his feet. "For which I am very grateful, Sir Basil. I'll have to devise something as an antidote first, I'm thinking, because I've already used the drug on myself as a test. So have two other people. That was before the Government proved so adamant."

"You—you mean you've actually doomed yourself to die in ten years?" Sir Basil exclaimed, amazed. "But I understood your experiments had been carried out on piglets!"

"And humans. I did not mention that. However, I have it on reliable scientific authority that I shall live to be ninety-three, so now I must see what I can do towards bringing that about. Good-day, Sir Basil."

Completely preoccupied, Royd left the building and returned home. By the time he had got there he had come to realize how delicate was the position. In duty bound he ought to tell Virginia and Gordon how things stood, but this he was reluctant to do, for both of them, with their now exceptionally resistant bodies, were coming to believe that they really had a chance—Gordon at least—of overcoming the fatal date of October 19, 2019. Gordon indeed had formed the conclusion that the Scanner had seen in his mind something that had since been changed. The Tensile-X liquid had not then been in the scheme of things. Royd, knowing that the Scanner had photographed something of which Gordon's brain must have been in possession, had not argued the matter.

And now? To explain the facts would bring back the old haunting fears, with added terror indeed, for if bone disintegration could occur in ten years, it would certainly be in a dangerously advanced state in eleven years—which now remained to 2026.

"Antidote," Royd muttered, prowling thoughtfully around the laboratory. "That is what I must find. There must be one, else how can I live to be ninety-three?"

So he set himself the immense task of trying to discover something to undo the work he had done, without ill effect on the persons concerned. Consequently, every time Gordon, Virgie, and baby Louise arrived they found him in the midst of profound experiments with all kinds of fluids and essences.

"What are you cooking up, Doc?" Gordon asked in wonder one day. "Something else for the benefit of humanity?"

Royd shook his head. "Not this time. I think we'll let humanity's benefit end with the synthetic Eye, which by now is world-famous. No, I'm just dabbling."

"Can you take time out to give Louise some of that Tensile-X?" Virgie asked. "We want her to grow up as strong as we are."

Royd looked at the infant in the girl's arms and reflected, then he shook his head.

"I don't advise it. I'm not sure how it might be assimilated at such tender years. Leave it awhile."

"Well, all right," Virgie agreed. "But not for too long. No use Gordon and I being so tough with possible immortality in sight, and Louise becoming just an ordinary woman."

Royd changed the subject. "And what have you been doing recently? Haven't seen much of you."

"Oh, just routine stuff," Gordon shrugged. "Frankly, I find things are getting monotonous. An everlasting stream of money from the 'Forever' watch and Spiritine can get boring. I've forgotten by now how much we're worth. Beyond just going down now and again to headquarters in London to sign papers, checks, and contracts—Virgie and I are finding things mighty slow."

"We made a diversion the other day," Virgie put in. "We went down into east London to take a look at the Zenith Glass Eye Company, which Blessington started."

"And how did you find it?"

"Derelict," Gordon answered in satisfaction. "Windows smashed in, doors half off, and the place up for sale cheap. Whatever business Blessington may have left behind for somebody else to keep going, it certainly fell flat on its face. The reason is obvious: the synthetic Eye."

"Naturally," Royd agreed, and glanced at his watch. "You will stay for lunch, of course?"

CHAPTER SIX

LOST ANTIDOTE

It was two o'clock when Gordon and Virginia departed, with vague references to a proposed world cruise to escape the vagaries of an English summer. Immediately Royd went back to work in the laboratory, following up a new line of reasoning which had taken him some weeks to perfect.

"Could be it," he breathed, eyeing the substance in a test tube. "Definite reactionary signs and complete elimination of the Tensile-X sediment."

He filled a hypodermic syringe with the stuff and then went into the adjoining animal department. Selecting one of his experimental piglets he gave it an injection, noted the time, and then returned to the laboratory to attend to routine matters. It would be some days before he could discover if his experiment was a success.

It was—and he could scarcely refrain from a whoop of joy as he examined the X-ray plates he had made of the piglet. It showed that the cariousness of the bone structure had been completely arrested. Since the injection there had been no deterioration, but there was also the fact that the cellular structure had lost its toughness and become more or less normal.

"A great might-have-been," Royd sighed. "An experiment in immortality which didn't quite come off. Maybe it will later, if I can overcome the bone trouble."

Without delay he gave himself an injection, and for two days afterwards was desperately sick. Then gradually he began to recover again and found that on his first attempt at shaving following his indisposition, the nick he gave himself with the razor drew blood. In the two short days he had undone the work of months of hardening.

Now came the problem to get Virginia and Gordon to take the antidote without them knowing what it was. And when they discovered their toughness had gone, as inevitably they would, what then? Their belief in being able to defeat the deadline day would be relentlessly shattered.

To this problem Royd gave a good deal of thought. He had the time, since he gathered that Gordon and Virginia were somewhere in the region of Bermuda in their private yacht, and it would be some months before they returned.

Yet despite his agile brain there was nothing he could conceive which would allow the antidote to be altered in any way—so at last, reluctantly, he resolved the only possible course—to tell Virgie outright how things stood and leave her to handle Gordon. That she was a woman of character with a profound love for Gordon were the two virtues upon which Royd decided to rely.

It was not until October that he had the opportunity to speak, and then he selected a time when Gordon was forced to be in London on business.

Virgie was quite surprised when Royd called upon her, for as a rule it was the other way round. She found him as apparently preoccupied as ever, but with an obvious something on his mind.

"It must be very important to bring you here, Doc," she said, smiling, as they settled in the great lounge. "And I hope it isn't too technical."

"No, Virgie, it isn't technical, but it is difficult. I have weighed it up for some months now how I would say this and now I have to do it I'm lost. Only thing I can do is to plunge. Briefly, Tensile-X is a dangerous drug unless counteracted. In ten or twelve years it can bring complete collapse to the bone structure."

Having had no lead-up to this pronouncement, Virgie just stared for a moment; then she found speech.

"You—you mean that this immortality business won't work? That this toughness we've developed isn't any use at all?"

"That's it. The Medical Association found it out first, and I have experimented since. The drug isn't complete. It produces hardness of the cells, but at the expense of the bones, and therefore it's deadly. The only solution is an antidote, which I have devised and taken myself. I'm back to normal, and you and Gordon must take the same course."

"But do you realize what it means?" Virgina demanded, "We've got so used to this condition, so sure it means Gordon can defeat that awful date—"

"Yes, yes, my dear, I know. Don't think I haven't given all that a tremendous lot of thought. That is why I'm telling you instead of Gordon. The reaction of such news on him, the way I tell it, might be disastrous. So I want you to do it. You can handle him better than I can."

For several moments the girl was silent, readjusting herself after the shock. Then she asked a question:

"I suppose the effect of the antidote will be noticeable? We'll discover that we can bruise ourselves as before? That we will not be able to withstand bullets, knives, and so on?"

"You will be back to normal," Royd said quietly. "And it has got to be done. Here is the antidote"—he took the small phial from his pocket—"and a hypodermic syringe. It merely requires injection. You'll be ill for two days afterwards, and then you'll pick up to find all the traces of toughness have gone."

"The end of our dreams and hopes!" Virgie looked hopelessly in front of her. "And I really thought we'd got the answer."

"So did I." Royd got to his feet. "I'm sorry, Virgie. I'm a meddling old idiot, I think. If only I had never got the idea for that infernal Scanner, all this trouble could have been avoided. Now I've made it worse by finding an apparent way of release, only to discover it doesn't work—I'll have to leave the rest to you. No more can I do."

"I realize that." Virginia forced a smile and shook

hands. "See you again, doctor."

After he had gone, she sat for a long time thinking the matter out, then finally she filled the syringe, gave herself an injection, and put the phial and syringe on one side. By the time Gordon arrived home again in the evening she was feeling pretty groggy, but she managed to keep up a pretence of light conversation.

Gordon kept looking at her during dinner, and again in the lounge afterwards, puzzled by the unusual color in her face and the brightness of her eyes.

"Anything wrong, Virgie?" he asked in concern. "You don't look so well."

"Oh, I'm all right." She made a tremendous effort to keep herself in focus. "Must be the effect of that stuff Dr. Royd said I should take. What he calls an 'equalizer' for Tensile-X."

"Equalizer?" Gordon looked puzzled. "You mean he's been here?"

"Whilst you were in town. He brought along some fluid and said we must take it. He's already done so. He's discovered that Tensile-X needs something extra in order to make it even out. I couldn't really grasp what he meant in the scientific sense, but anyway I gave myself an injection and you'd better do likewise."

"Oh?" Gordon's eyes followed the girl's gaze to the phial and syringe nearby; then he looked back at her. "But what does the stuff do? I can't see the need of it. I never felt better in my life, and the same could have been said for you when I left this morning. Now look at you!"

"Only reaction to the stuff," Virginia explained, breathing heavily. "Same sort of thing you get after inoculation."

"And when the equalizing business has run its course, what happens?"

"As far as I can tell we still live for a very long time, but the iron-hard effect on the cells is changed. We become almost normal, to all intents and purposes, but longevity is in no wise altered."

Virginia hated herself for her lies, but she could think of no other way round the business. It made it extra hard to have Gordon's thoughtful eyes fixed upon her. Finally he turned to the telephone and picked it up, rang Dr. Royd's number. In the receiver there came the constant dialing tone but no answer came forth.

"That's queer!" Gordon gave a frown and returned the instrument to its rest. "No reply! Even if the Doc is out, one of the staff ought to be able to answer."

"Why bother about that?" Virginia asked. "Don't you believe what I have told you?"

"Of course I do. Why not? Only I'd like the scientific facts a little clearer—and I don't like the look of you. Royd had better come and see you. Meantime, I think you should go to bed."

"Yes, perhaps I should." Virginia struggled to her feet, and then gasped a little as she found herself tottering forward. Just in time Gordon caught her in his arms.

"What sort of stuff Royd calls this I don't know," he said bitterly, "but he's got some explaining to do."

He bore the girl upstairs, helped her to get to bed, and then told the domestic staff to keep an eye on her. This done, he hurried quickly into his hat and coat, then, bethinking himself, he collected the bottle of liquid and pushed it in his pocket. In a few minutes he was on his way to Dr. Royd's, giving the car all it had got through the dank gloom of the October night. It was as he came within sight of the Larches that he gave a start. There was a redness pulsating the sky above the treetops, and the more he weighed up the direction the more certain he became that only the Larches could account for it.

A moment or two later his worst fears were confirmed. As he raced his car round a bend in the lane the full view of the Larches burst upon his vision, flames roaring into the night from both the residence itself and the annexed buildings.

Gordon swept the car up the driveway, saw it was impossible to make an entrance by the front doorway, and so raced round to the rear laboratory door that he knew so well. It was burning furiously and collapsed at the kick he gave it. He pulled off his overcoat and wrapped it round his head for protection, then plunged into the smoke and flames beyond.

"Dr. Royd!" he yelled. "Doc, where are you?"

There was no answer. His eyes smarting, Gordon looked about him. The chemicals in the laboratory were burning fiercely, emitting all kinds of mephitic odors and half-choking him, but in the center of the space the flames had not yet reached and it was here that he beheld Dr. Royd, lying apparently unconscious, firmly bound round the ankles and wrists, a length of cord being secured to one of the stout wooden legs of the bench.

Gordon threw off the coat hampering his movements and pulled out his penknife. In one slash he severed the cord from the bench, then picking up the scientist in his arms he blundered with him through the open doorway and into the cold night air. Royd began to stir slightly as the clear atmosphere revived him.

"Staff—inside," he whispered thickly. "Try—try and free them—"

Gordon gave a horrified look and then raced to the rear regions of the great residence, but he could tell even as he did so that he was beaten. The whole mass of the Larches had become transformed into skeleton walls, looming black against the raging fire within them. To save anybody in the midst of such a holocaust was quite impossible.

Grim-faced and sweating he returned to where he had left Royd, to discover that villagers, attracted by the blaze, had arrived on the scene. In the distance could be heard the ever-increasing clang of bells as fire-engines from Reading evidently summoned by the villagers, hurtled to the scene.

"I'm taking Dr. Royd to my home," Gordon told one of the men. "You know me? Gordon Fryer?"

"I do that," the man answered.

"Right. Apparently some of the domestic staff have been trapped in the fire."

Gordon wasted no more time. Helping the now recovered but shaken scientist across the grass he finally settled him in the car and then began to drive back home.

"What the devil happened?" Gordon demanded, puzzled. "Who tied you up like that, Doc?"

"Four men," Royd answered. "They were so sure of the fact I'd be killed that they admitted that they were acting for Blessington."

"What! You mean they deliberately set fire to your place, and tried to kill you?"

"Just that. I'm afraid they did kill the domestic staff. They told me they'd trussed them all up in the kitchen. A horrible, ghastly business!" Royd whispered, feeling for the spectacles that he had lost in the confusion. "There was just nothing I could do. They walked in on me from the rear door of the lab and that was that. Evidently they had been keeping track of my movements for some time."

"But why should Blessington's cronies want to attack you?" Gordon demanded. "I'd have thought they'd have been more likely to tackle me."

"They will in time! They as good as promised that. You'll have to watch out for yourself, Gordon, unless the Police can nail them. I've a pretty good idea what each man looked like."

Gordon was silent for a while, driving swiftly onwards.

"Lucky I came over when I did," he said presently. "Virgie has been taken ill because of some kind of drug you had her take. I want to know all about it. I mean this stuff here—"

Gordon dropped a hand to his jacket pocket and then swore.

"I'd forgotten," he said. "I had the stuff in my overcoat and dropped it somewhere in the flames back at your place. I'm talking about the equalizer."

"The—oh, the equalizer!" Royd frowned to himself, deciding that that must be the name Virgie had given the liquid. "Didn't she make it clear to you why you ought to take the stuff?"

"As near as she could, yes, but she's not to be expected to recite the formula. I can't see why it should be so necessary to reduce toughness and yet retain longevity. I prefer to keep both."

Royd could be forgiven for his silence as he tried to weigh up what kind of a story Virginia must have told.

"So Virgie's ill?" he asked at length. "I warned her that would happen. It happened to me, too. Natural outcome. In a couple of days she'll be fine, just as you will."

"How do you mean—as I will? I haven't taken the stuff yet, and I'm not going to until I'm sure it's imperative. Don't you realize I'm relying on my toughness to beat the Date?"

"Of course, but—you haven't taken a dose yet?"

"No. I brought the remainder over to you, and now I've lost it in the fire somewhere. If it's vitally essential, you'll have to make up some more for me—but honestly I'd prefer not to take it."

The dim light of the car was sufficient to hide Royd's look of alarm. With considerable effort he kept his voice at its usual level.

"I can't make up any more, Gordon. The stuff it was made from was a special distillation. The basis of it was a root I found in South America many years ago, and I could no more find that again than go back and pick a particular blade of grass. There was plenty of it, but it's gone in the fire, like everything else."

"Oh?" Gordon drove on for a while. "Well, perhaps it is just as well. I don't want to change things."

Royd put finger and thumb to his eyes and Gordon glanced at him. "Feeling bad, Doc? We'll soon fix you up."

In another ten minutes he was home and helped the scientist into the lounge. After a glass of brandy he revived considerably, but the startled look had not left his eyes. He was still trying to absorb the numbing fact that the antidote had been taken by Virginia and himself, but that Gordon had all unwittingly walked straight into a trap.

The next day Virginia was much better and Royd himself, after a night's sleep, was completely recovered—though very much lost without his home and laboratory, or a spare pair of spectacles. Finally he decided to go into Reading and have an emergency pair made. To the matter of the antidote he did not refer again, because there was nothing he could say. The whole thing had been wiped out and he had still to break the news to Virginia somehow.

During the morning a fire brigade representative called with the news that the Larches had been completely gutted.

"Not a thing left," the representative said. "Our men were called much too late. I understand from the police who were present this morning that the whole matter was arson and attempted murder?"

"Exactly," Gordon assented grimly. "I informed the police last night—and murder was more than attempted: it succeeded! Some of the domestic staff were trapped."

"That's true. We found charred bodies. We did all we could."

Gordon nodded and a few minutes later the representative left. Half an hour after his departure Chief-inspector Bland, Gordon's particular friend from Scotland Yard, turned up.

"It's Dr. Royd I'm looking for," he explained. "I want a description of the four men who attacked him, or better still, he'd help if he came down to the Yard and looked through our Records Department to see if he recognizes any well-known fire-raisers."

"Dr. Royd's in Reading at the moment," Gordon responded. "In any case I'd hardly think that the friends of Blessington would have criminal records. Be a waste of time looking for their photographs, wouldn't it?"

"One of them must have been an experienced fire-raiser," Bland declared resolutely. "The fire assessors and our own experts have tooth-combed those ruins, and there's no doubt but that the whole thing had been engineered for some time. In what remains of the cellars we found all the traces of a fire-raiser's tricks. Anyway, the fact remains that I have warrants to take out. Murder has been done. How soon will Dr. Royd be back?"

"Any time. He went to see about some spectacles. Best thing I can do is to ask him to call on you at the Yard. I'll see he's driven over."

Bland nodded. "Good!"

"And one thing more," Gordon added. "I want police protection for myself, my wife, and my home, and indeed for Dr. Royd too, if it comes to that. These men know by now that he escaped last night's fire, the papers are full of it, so they may try again here."

"Just what," Bland asked, "is their motive? I gathered over the phone that you believe these men are friends of Blessington. I suppose it is the fact that Blessington got jail and he is trying to get his revenge through these criminal associates of his."

"Partly that. I also think that the Fryer Eye, of which everybody knows these days, is responsible. It put Blessington's business right out of action, assuming it continued after he had been sent to jail."

"It continued all right: I had a man check up on it to our own satisfaction."

Gordon spread his hands. "Then the explanation's as I have given it. Blessington has lost his business and his liberty, and obviously blames Dr. Royd and me for it since we were jointly concerned in the creation of the synthetic eye. All right, inspector, I won't take up any more of your time. Just arrange that police protection for me and I'll see Dr. Royd calls on you without loss of time."

Gordon was as good as his word, and dispatched the scientist to the City the moment he returned from Reading. He had hardly done so and was thinking of a rather lonely lunch when to his surprise Virginia came into the lounge, pale, but looking generally better than she had been on the previous evening.

"You shouldn't be about so soon, my dear," Gordon told her, making her armchair comfortable.

"Oh, I'll live," she said dryly. "Don't forget the Scanner!"

"I wish I could."

"Sorry, Gordon: that was stupid of me! I had to come down to find out how things are progressing. Any news about the fire at Dr. Royd's?"

Gordon gave the details and finally Virginia looked at him curiously. "It surprises me you arc standing up so well under the equalizer fluid. I expected to find you going under as I did."

"I didn't take any," he growled. "For one thing I didn't see any real reason for it, and for, another I couldn't even if I had wanted. I lost my bottle of stuff in the fire and the Doc can't make any more."

"What!" Virginia stared at him fixedly, but he merely shrugged.

"Why so bothered? I prefer things the way they are. I like my toughness, anyway, and I don't intend to part with it. I consider it my insurance against the Scanner."

"But, Gordon—"

"Yes?"

"Nothing," Virgie said quietly, but the look in her eyes was beyond Gordon's understanding.

* * * * * * *

The quandary into which both Dr. Royd and Virginia had been thrown showed no sign of solving itself as the days and then the weeks passed by. Gordon had taken Dr. Royd into his own home and had a laboratory built and equipped for him, partly as return for the old man's generosity in the earlier years, and here Royd would have worked contentedly but for the everlasting niggling worry in the back of his mind.

Time and again he and Virgie had the matter out between themselves, exploring every possibility, but the relentless fact remained that duplication of the antidote was impossible with the basic ingredients destroyed, since all the money on Earth lavished on expeditions to Central America could not guarantee that the particular root substance Royd had used could ever be found.

The alternative was to tell Gordon the truth and then what? The frontier of courage behind which he sheltered himself; his obvious ever-growing conviction that his immense physical resistance would enable him to sidetrack the Scanner, would be wiped out and a hopeless mental state would ensue.

"No, that isn't the answer," Virginia said bitterly, at the close of one of these confabs. "If it has to happen, better it does so at the time than for him to be warned about it years in advance."

"So I think," Royd sighed. "I realize, my dear, just how you feel, and the measure of your unhappiness is also the measure of mine. In producing the antidote, the one thing I thought might solve our problem, I have created the very thing which will make the end come about! There are times when the inscrutability of Destiny is beyond understanding."

Since it had been agreed that nothing should be said, Gordon was left in ignorance, although it was plain from his manner that at times he did wonder at the moodiness of his wife and Dr. Royd.

In other directions events moved with considerable rapidity. Dr. Royd's identification of one man in the quartet who had attacked him had given Chief-Inspector Bland all the information he needed, and within a month all four men were in custody. Which seemed to end the final threat of the utterly defeated and malignant Blessington. Certainly no attempts were made on Gordon's own life or that of Virgie, or little Louise, so it appeared the menace had been stopped at the source.

The weeks became months, and out of the almost chaotic and frenzied endeavor of the earlier years there began to emerge a complacent peace, as far as Gordon was concerned anyway. He was strong, wealthy, had a devoted wife and a fast-growing daughter, all states of mind contributing his belief that he would even yet prove the Scanner wrong. He spent his time traveling as the mood moved him, always taking Virgie and Louise with him, spending only enough time in England to attend to essentials of business, and leaving Dr. Royd more or less in charge and free to dabble as he chose.

Then, two years after the fire at the Larches, Gordon found himself unexpectedly caught out, and it came as a rude shock and a grim reminder.

It was on a sultry day in June, the first summer he had elected to stay at home for a change. He was seated in the lounge the French windows open to the lawn upon which poured the blazing tide of sunlight. Outside on the grass Virgie was playing with little Louise, rolling her brightly colored ball back and forth. Suddenly the child seized it and threw it. It sailed straight through the open windows and landed in the midst of Gordon's newspaper as he held it up. Smiling, he got to his feet and inwardly cursed his girth. Tossing the ball back to Louise he held up his hand for her to throw the ball back and there he froze, startled.

"Virgie," he half whispered. "Virgie, come here a moment."

Surprised, she got up and hurried to him, the child blissfully continuing playing.

"What is it?" Virginia asked, her face anxious.

"The—the fourth photograph just came true at that moment." Gordon lowered his arm and pressed finger and thumb to his eyes. "Oh, why in heaven's name do these things keep coming to pass? So naturally and so unexpectedly! What—what year is it?" he demanded, in sudden panic.

"Why, 2010, of course!"

Gordon picked up the newspaper. "And the date is June tenth. Yes, that's it! I'd forgotten all about it. That blasted Scanner again!"

Virginia was silent, vaguely horror-stricken at this new evidence of immutable law. Gordon left her for a moment and hurried to his study. He returned with the photographs in their manilla folder. He had brought them into his own home when he had taken possession, so at least they had escaped the fire.

"That's the one," he said, and indicated the picture of the lawn. "Yes. Clothes are identical, the striped play-ball, and everything! It might have been taken a few hours ago instead of four years ago."

Virginia nodded slowly. "Shall we look at the others which are still supposed to come?"

"No!" Gordon shut the file decisively. "Anything but that! I'm not depicted again until September, 2013, and that has something to do with the BOA. Virgie, I'm getting scared!" He stared fixedly into the sunlight.

Her hand rested on his arm. "Don't, Gordon! Getting scared won't do any good, but I do think it is time we planned things so that the other photographs cannot come true."

"How, for instance?"

"I don't know off-hand; takes thinking about, but just consider: had we been more alert concerning today and made note of the date, we could have gone for a run in the country—anywhere away from here, and so stopped that incident from taking place."

"But we didn't, Virgie—we didn't! That's what makes the whole business so damnable! We walk right into these things without realizing it until it's over. It's terrifying!"

This time Virgie was silent. She had, if anything, an even greater mental load to carry than Gordon himself, and no matter how she viewed the problem she could see no way to solve it.

"We'll watch it next time," she said finally, with a brave little smile, and considered it best to let the matter drop there.

Gordon did not refer to it again either, not even to the constantly preoccupied Dr. Royd as, growing visibly older with the years, he still dabbled with endless but more or less useless experiments in an effort to undo the tangle his Tensile-X had started.

It was indeed this visible sign of ageing which impressed Gordon quite a deal, though he did not say anything about it openly until January of the following year—2011. Then, one winter's night, when Louise had been put to bed and the conditions seemed favorable for conversation, Gordon brought the subject up, jocularly at first.

"Still convinced you'll live to be ninety-three, Doc?"

Royd peered over his spectacles, on the defensive immediately, whilst Virginia gazed into the fire and listened with every nerve keyed up.

"The Scanner said so," Royd shrugged. "So I say so, too."

"True. But when you invented Tensile-X you said

that you might have made a mistake in the Scanner somewhere, which would enable me to cheat the fatal date. If in my case, why not yours?"

"Could be," Royd admitted. "But where is all this leading?"

"It's leading to this: Tensile-X doesn't seem to be having the effect on you that it should. You reckoned two hundred years: the Scanner said ninety-three. From the look of it I can't see you living another twenty years, not by any stretch of the imagination."

"To become ninety-three I shan't need to live twenty years."

Gordon started. "You won't? How do you mean?"

"Simply that I'm eighty-three now. You have always assumed me to be much younger because I've worn well, until just recently. Now it's beginning to show."

"Eighty-three!" Virginia exclaimed. "I'd never have guessed it, Doc!"

"But it ought not to show!" Gordon insisted. "That's the whole point. Tensile-X ought to keep you at the place you approximately were at when you first took it. How otherwise can you run the expected course for two hundred years or so?"

Royd said nothing. He gazed pensively into the fire.

"There are a lot of things I do not understand," Gordon continued slowly, after a moment. "You and Virgie are both becoming older as the years march on, but not I. I am as tough and fit as the day I took Tensile-X, and I feel okay. You two changed when you tried that equalizing stuff. What on Earth did you have to bother with it for? From the look of you it spoiled the effect."

"Possibly so," Royd sighed. "With a drug like that the effects are unpredictable. As I feel at the moment I certainly shan't live to be two hundred, or even one, and you mustn't ever forget that disease has not been reckoned with."

Gordon looked sharply at Virginia, just in time to see her expression as she gazed at Royd. It was one difficult to analyze, half horror and half expectancy.

"There is one fact that I cannot get away from," Gordon went on deliberately. "I have had the feeling all the time that both of you are holding something back. I don't know what, and maybe it is intended for my own good that you do. But it's there and I don't altogether like it. It wouldn't by any chance be that both of you have discovered you've lost the power which Tensile-X gave you and don't wasn't to admit it to me, would it?"

"Yes it would," Virginia said, seizing the chance. "That's just it. We didn't know how to tell you, but since you've brought it up yourself, that's the answer. Consider our position, having to tell you that you may live to be two hundred whereas nobody else in the world will."

Gordon was silent for a long time; then he said, half jocularly, "Well, there it is! Made something of a mess of the equalizer, Doc, didn't you? Better to have stopped as you were like me."

Abruptly he dropped the conversation and the tension relaxed.

Virginia had taken the line of least resistance and she felt that her lie had been justified. Apparently Gordon was satisfied with the explanation, since he did not refer to it again that night. His attitude, however, slowly began to change. There was a bitterness in his expression and less tolerance towards Virgie and Dr. Royd. It was as though he secretly felt they had dodged the issue of immortality or at least two hundred years of life and left him to carry the load alone, which in his private estimation, would be worse than dying eight years hence.

So the almost changeless years drifted by: 2011, 2012, and so into 2013, with Louise five years of age and every bit as pretty as her mother. Gordon was well aware that he had a 'photographic date' on September 6th of this year, and as early as June he began to make preparations to evade it. Royd was also called into the 'conference', which Gordon held with Virgie one evening in mid-summer in the grounds.

"We're going to Australia," he said, "and shall not return until January next year. I've made all the arrangements, and no matter what happens I shall definitely not appear before a BOA gathering on September sixth."

"I'm with you," Virgie said promptly. "You haven't even been asked to appear before such a gathering as yet, so it certainly can't be said by the BOA that you're running out on them."

"Just what I was thinking. We'll get well out of the way before they can send me an invitation. By

September we'll be on the other side of the world. Louise will come with us, of course, so we'll have no ties back here at all. How about you, Doc? Care to come?"

"Nothing I'd like better."

"Then it's settled," Gordon decided. "I'll notify Captain Harslake that we'll commence our cruise a week from today. That will give him ample time to get the yacht prepared."

Gordon wasted no more time. He carried out his plan to the last detail and on June 10th he, Virgie, Louise, and Royd embarked. For Royd it was a new and interesting experience; but for Gordon and Virginia it was merely a repetition of the kind of thing they had enjoyed many times in their married life.

The route selected was the longest Gordon could suggest. From Southampton to Lisbon, thence to Madeira and Gambia on the West African coast. So down to Cape Town, then the long five-thousand mile journey to Australia.

"This," Gordon said on the third day out, and in the midst of perfect summer weather, "will really put the Scanner to shame, Doc. I suppose we could have done it sooner if we'd thought of it."

"Possibly," Royd conceded, disinclined to discuss the matter.

The reason was understandable. The sun was hot, the sea glassy, and the deck chairs wonderfully comfortable. It was one of those drowsy moments when nothing particularly mattered. Presently however, the peace was broken as Captain Harslake came into view.

"Sorry to interrupt you, Mr. Fryer," he apologized, "but could you spare me a moment?"

"What about, Captain?" Gordon opened an eye lazily. "Can't it wait?"

"I'm afraid not, sir. And it's confidential. If you'd be good enough to step to my cabin."

With a sigh Gordon struggled out of the deck chair, gave a shrug to Virginia and Royd, and then followed the captain along the deck and into his cabin.

"I would prefer, sir," Harslake said, pouring out drinks, "that we don't undertake this trip to Australia."

Gordon looked astonished. "You'd prefer? Why not, pray?"

"I don't think our engines will stand the trip. We've been on a good many voyages in the last few years, sir, and it's time we drydocked for an overhaul. I wasn't aware they were in such a bad condition until we began this trip."

Gordon swallowed his drink, listening at the same time to the distant buried rumbling from the engine room.

"I don't detect anything wrong with the rhythm," he commented.

"You won't sir, yet. But the chief engineer informs me that our main driving shaft is in bad shape. If we ever get to Australia it will be a miracle. If we do get that far we should remain until the overhaul can be completed."

"Easy enough," Gordon said. "We'll do that. Carry

on and overhaul when we arrive."

"If we do. What if we break down in mid-ocean? In our present condition it could easily happen."

Gordon put down his glass impatiently. "Why the devil was I not told of all this before we started? As captain you should have looked into it. Had I known I'd have flown to Australia."

"I'm not the chief engineer, sir," Harslake defended himself. "Until he told me, I was satisfied that we were absolutely seaworthy. My suggestion is that we put in at Lisbon for an overhaul."

"Very well," Gordon agreed, after reflection. "We can stay in Lisbon until after the job's done. How long will it take?"

"Depends. I reckon a month."

"Right. Telegraph for reservations in Lisbon, will you?"

Gordon left the cabin, looking vaguely annoyed. The hitch in the proceedings had disturbed him considerably; still, just as long as he remained sufficiently far away from England that was all that concerned him.

"What's wrong?" Virginia asked him, as he returned to his deck chair.

"Engine trouble. We'll have to put in at Lisbon, and maybe stay there for a month. Nothing to worry about, Lisbon's as good as anywhere as far as we're concerned."

Virginia nodded slowly, her eyes on the playing figure of Louise as she gamboled about the deck. Like Gordon, Virgie was thinking of the hitch in the perfect plan and she could not rid herself of the fear it engendered.

Captain Harslake's forebodings were, however, realized much more quickly than even he, or the chief engineer, had expected. That same night the calm weather changed abruptly to rain and wind, with the result that extra strain was thrown on the engines, and off the coast of northern Spain a breakdown occurred.

By radio and rockets Harslake notified his position, meanwhile doing his utmost by means of a jury rig fore and aft to keep the helpless vessel from plunging on the Spanish coast. In this his seamanship was successful, and by dawn the weather had calmed again, bringing to view a tramp steamer answering the S.O.S.

To Gordon, matters of seamanship did not mean a thing, so all he could do was wait for some information, lounging about the deck with Virginia and Louise meanwhile. Royd never appeared until lunchtime, anyway.

"Nice thing!" Gordon muttered, glaring at the battered old tramp nearby. "A luxury yacht, and we're stuck out here like an old salmon tin. Makes you sick!"

"At least we managed to get somebody who can help us out, so I suppose we ought to be grateful for that," said Virgie.

Gordon made no answer. His face was grim—not so much because of the incident itself but because of the utter disruption of his plans. Where Virgie managed to control her feelings, he found it next to impossible to do so.

It was towards noon when at last Captain Harslake sent word that he would be glad if Mr. Fryer would step to his cabin, so Gordon went, to find Harslake and the bearded skipper of the tramp present along with the chief engineer.

"Nothing else for it, Mr. Fryer, but to be towed back to England," Harslake said, wasting no time.

"To England? I thought you said Lisbon!"

"That was if we could make it, sir, and we didn't! Captain Rutter here is headed for Southampton and he could take us along with him."

"If to Southampton, why not to Lisbon?" Gordon demanded, but the bearded skipper shook his head.

"I can't do that, sir. I'm on a time schedule and I'd be fired if I landed back in port some weeks behind time. Stuff is on Government contract."

"I'll make it worth your while to take us to Lisbon," Gordon said, and at that the chief engineer spoke.

"It wouldn't be any use, Mr. Fryer. We need a complete new driving shaft and Lisbon couldn't supply it. This yacht isn't using standard marine engines, remember: they were specially built on Clydeside. The only possible way is to get towed back to England. After that it's easy."

"Not to me," Gordon muttered, then realizing the men were exchanging puzzled glances he pulled himself together. "Very well, I shall have to bow to your expert opinion. Get on with the job, gentlemen."

He left the cabin with impatient strides and returned to where Virginia was playing with Louise on the deck.

Briefly he made the situation clear to her.

"So there it is," he finished bitterly. "Back to England whether we like it or not!"

"It'll only be early July," Virginia said. "We can get the repairs done and then start off again."

"Not if I know it. The moment this yacht's back home I'm chartering a plane and we'll fly immediately to Melbourne. I don't intend to stay in England a day longer than I can help."

CHAPTER SEVEN

DESTINY

For all his planning, however, Gordon found himself baulked. Once back in Britain he just could not immediately depart and leave the matter of the broken-down yacht to Captain Harslake and the chief engineer. Perforce he stayed or a fortnight giving his sanction to the repairs that must be done; then he made his belated preparations for departure by plane to Australia.

The one thing marring his plans now was a peculiar lassitude on the part of little Louise, and her disinclination to eat or play. At first neither he or Virginia paid particular attention to it, believing it to be some child's ailment or other, but when the condition rapidly worsened they realized something had got to be done. Whatever happened, no matter how tangled their own fates in the web of Destiny, Louise was their first concern. So Gordon abandoned his plans for the time being and summoned the best child specialist Harley Street could produce.

"Not serious," the specialist reassured the troubled parents, when his diagnosis was complete. "But it will take a considerable time to straighten it out."

"What is the trouble?" Gordon asked, his voice dull.

"Well, to cut out all the technical phraseology, I'd say an overdose of sunlight. Where have you had her recently?"

"On board my yacht."

"Mmm. In a good deal of sunlight without a hat?"

"As she's so used to the sun I didn't think there was any harm in it," Virginia said.

"On the contrary, Mrs. Fryer, you cannot be too careful with a child of her years. Ultraviolet can sometimes be dangerous in excess. That briefly is her trouble. A form of severe latent sunstroke with slight paralysis, but there's no danger at all providing we take her in hand immediately. She must be removed to my sanatorium for treatment."

"And how long will the treatment take?" Gordon asked.

The specialist reflected, not so much upon the requirements of the case but also upon the fact that Gordon Fryer was a fabulously wealthy man.

"At the least I'd say four months," he replied finally. "No use rushing these things, you understand. You want her perfectly right when we're finished."

"Naturally," Virgie agreed promptly, casting Gordon a look.

The lines of his jaw tightened, but still the thought uppermost in his mind was the welfare of his daughter. "Very well," he assented. "Please make the necessary arrangements."

"And you will both be on call, I hope? Very often a

child requires its parents, and I must feel that you can be brought at a moment's notice should the occasion arise."

"We'll be on hand," Gordon promised, and satisfied, the specialist departed. When the door had closed behind the manservant, Gordon gave Virginia a look. It said far more than words could have done.

"Back where we started!" he said at last. "It's no use, Virgie, this thing can't be fought. That's obvious."

"In this instance, yes," she admitted. "But it's not the last call, Gordon. You can still go to Australia by yourself and leave me to handle Louise if need be."

"What! Leave Louise when the sound of my voice might save her life in a sudden crisis? Not likely!" Gordon moved tempestuously. "Oh, what's the use of kidding ourselves? This ghastly business is running to schedule and there's nothing we can do to stop it! I'd better go and tell the Doc how things are, and that the Australian trip is off."

Off it definitely was, nor did Gordon make the least effort to leave the country. The recent events had forced him to adapt a completely fatalistic attitude about the whole business, and thereafter he seemed to live from day to day in a kind of daze. Apart from his essential business calls and regular visits to Louise with Virgie beside him, he seemed to take very little interest in things in general, but even he could not remain entirely oblivious to the fact that, as August came in, there were newspaper, television, and radio announcements to the effect that the Fryer Eye had just reached the million mark and had restored an afflicted multitude to perfect vision.

Gordon accepted the news stolidly, realizing what it meant. The first signs of September 6th were beginning to show themselves. On September 1st the President of the British Optical Association sent a cordial invitation to Gordon, asking him to be the guest of honor at the annual banquet on September 6th, prepared to make a speech on the events that had led up to the creation of the Fryer Eye.

"So here it is," he said whimsically, showing Virginia the card. "And I can't get out of it without insulting the entire faculty. To save my life or prove the Scanner wrong I would absent myself, but—" He stopped and considered.

"Well, as you said earlier, it isn't the last call yet. I'd better go—"

"In evening dress, of course?"

"Naturally. Oh, I see what you mean! The vow we made that I would never wear it. In this instance it can't signify. No way out, Virgie. I must go." And since the banquet was televised, Virginia was able to see the welcome he received and hear the splendid speech he gave, in which he insisted that the credit must be shared with the famous Dr. Royd. The old man, also watching and listening at Virginia's side, smiled faintly at the eulogy; then abruptly to the television screen came a changed position, and there was a brief scene with Gordon well in the forefront of the dais, officials around him, and the pennant of the BOA looming blurredly to the rear.

"That's it, Virgie," Royd said quietly. "The scene the Scanner photographed."

"I know." Her voice sounded faraway. "Doc, tell me: are you still of the opinion that we shouldn't tell him about the effect of Tensile-X? That it will fail him as far as bone structure is concerned in another six or seven years."

"I am still of that opinion," he conceded. "It could do no good. He is a worried enough man already: more would not exactly help. But I certainly think that the six years which remain before the fated date should be very carefully planned in a last desperate effort to beat the relentless predictions which, so far, have all come true."

For Dr. Royd it was more or less easy to say what should be done for, having arrived at the point where he could see no further way round the problem, he had adopted a certain grim resignation. Not so Virginia. Despite the forecasted collapse of Tensile-X before many years had passed, despite the warning of the Scanner, she still managed to smile and weave schemes whereby Gordon might at least stand a fighting chance when the fatal year came round. Just prove the Scanner wrong in the smallest particular and the spell would be broken.

Once he returned home after the eulogy of the BOA with a certificate which made him a Fellow of the World Society of Optics, Gordon reverted to his former somber mood, attending to business, welcoming the return of the completely recovered Louise in late September, and doing his best all the time to studiously avoid mentioning the matter which was buried deepest in his mind.

In the summer of 2014 he at last took the sea voyage to Australia, chiefly to restore Louise to full health, keeping her protected from the sun en route, and in this measure he succeeded, but as far as he was concerned he returned in exactly the same mood as that in which he left, despondent and resentful with the expression of a man fighting a hopeless battle.

It seemed even more ironical to him that in every other field he had nothing but success. The money still rolled in, and the Spiritine Corporation had by now completely supplanted the old-time petroleum companies. As far as the 'Forever' Watch was concerned, it was now about the only form of watch worn by men and women throughout the world, but true to his original arrangement with Virginia he had never altered the design—nor did he intend to.

Indeed, in the years 2015, 2016, 2017, and 2018 he could not have had anything more, except peace of mind, and the lack of this made everything else utterly empty and devoid of meaning. Then, as 2019 came in, he began in January to consider seriously the problem that lay ahead. The sands were running out!

Virginia was now the more worried because at any moment the strength of Tensile-X ought to fail, and anything could happen. Yet the Scanner had forecast October, so if it were true nothing disastrous could happen until then. Above all things, that month must be completely sidetracked, and certainly the fated date of October 19.

It was in August when Gordon received a shock. The papers announced, in an inconspicuous column, that Henry Blessington, ex-glass eye manufacturer, had been released from jail after serving his full sentence. He had had to serve out the whole of the twelve years, because of his association with the fire raisers.

"Which means," Gordon said at breakfast one hot morning, "that he'll probably try and shift heaven and earth to get at me. I wrecked his business, got him landed in jail, and was the cause of his friends being arrested. Yes, I have the impression he'll stop at nothing. And you, too, Doc, had better watch your step."

The old scientist shrugged. "As far as I am concerned I rarely leave the house or the laboratory, thanks to your generosity, so Blessington will not have much chance to get at me. Just the same I think you'd do worse, Gordon, than ask for police protection."

"I most certainly will, this very morning."

It was promptly given when put in the hands of Chief-Inspector Bland, plainclothes men keeping a watch particularly on the movements of Louise and Virginia when they were out of the house. Gordon for his part was quite sure enough of his own toughness to feel convinced he could defeat anything Blessington was likely to attempt.

It was in mid-September that Gordon received a

letter from the Incorporated Society of Inventors, and it came just at the time he was planning an indefinite holiday abroad, alone, especially to escape the fated month. When he had read the letter through his lips tightened and he handed it to Virgie. It read:

September 10th, 2019.

My dear Mr. Fryer,

Unanimously, the Incorporated Society of Inventors has agreed that you are the leading inventor of the present decade, chiefly on account of your 'Spiritine', to say nothing of your famous Fryer Eye, and collaboration with Dr. Royd in the creation of the infallible 'Forever Watch'. You are most respectfully asked to attend our annual dinner on the night of October 19th next at 8 p.m., where, as the guest of honor, you will receive the National Award of Merit.

Most sincerely,

The Chief Secretary

"Well, that is the date," Virginia said, handing the letter back. "What happens now? You'll refuse, of course?"

"I can't," Gordon answered seriously. "The Society of Inventors is the most powerful body of its kind in the country. If I refused this invitation, they could make things mighty difficult for me. I can't afford to take that risk."

"But Gordon, you are worth millions, and this is the fatal date! You must do everything possible to avoid stepping into the trap."

"I shall. As for my millions, they'll vanish like smoke if I don't keep up the sales, and what kind of heritage would that be for Louise? No, I'll accept this invitation but I will plan everything so that I don't sideslip. That is what we have got to do now. Be a good soul and get the photographs of the last date, will you? They're in the study."

Virginia nodded and hurried from the library. In a moment or two she was back and Gordon carefully studied the photographs, the one of the fight and the other of his presumed death. Now he was brought face to face with the issue he found he was able to view it with cold detachment.

"In this fight scene I look to be wearing a homburg hat," he said. "Hard to tell in silhouette but in regard to the death scene I've no clothes resembling this hideous check overcoat and soft hat. So that is one point we can prove wrong. I have a dress suit, of course, and for the dinner I shall wear it, but I shall wear my brown tweeds before the dinner and after it, for my journey to and from London. I shall go in the car and avoid the train sequence. Again, I do not wear a wristwatch, and never shall, and I doubt if a watch like this is even in existence these days. That takes care of a number of points which can upset the picture."

"Right," Virgie said, "but I'm still scared."

"We'll get round it!" Gordon's face was grim. "It has got to be done because it's the last throw of the dice."

"Yes," Virgie whispered. "The last throw."

And she could not rid herself thereafter of the vast depression that weighed upon her soul. Dr. Royd, knowing what had been arranged, could see no reason why the meticulous attention to detail should not throw the scanner's forecast out of court. There remained only the unknown factor, the inscrutable something, which often brings disaster.

So finally October 19th dawned. Until early evening Gordon spent his time at home, making sure he had everything arranged to circumvent disaster; then at six o'clock, as the dreary twilight was closing in, he took his leave of Virginia and Louise.

"God bless you, dearest," Virginia whispered, kissing him profusely. "I shall not stop praying all the time you are away."

"Me too, daddy," Louise said quickly, as Gordon scooped her up in his arms.

He gave a brief rugged smile. "I'll be back in the morning, safe and sound." He gave a taut smile as he put the child down. "Then a new life will begin and the Scanner will be proven forever a liar! Well, goodbye, Doc."

"Good luck, my boy. It's a long time since I prayed, but I'll do my best."

Gordon laughed and stepped into the limousine as

the chauffeur held open the door. A moment later the car started off down the drive and swept out into the open road beyond the residence. Darkness was falling rapidly now and Gordon looked out upon it pensively, a myriad thoughts chasing through his mind. He wondered now how he had ever survived all the years that had led up to this particular day. It had dominated his whole life. Now it was here and he would defeat it!

Satisfied that he had made every possible move on the chessboard of his fate, he relaxed in the soft upholstery. Reading was passed in a blaze of light, then after sweeping through a long stretch of darkened countryside Wokingham was left behind and Ascot was ahead. But there was something amiss with the limousine. The engine was jerking queerly despite all the chauffeur's efforts to correct the fault. The trouble finally crystallized when a rising gradient in the road was struck and the car sighed to a halt.

"What is it?" Gordon demanded, pushing back the glass partition. "Norton, what's wrong?"

"Not sure, sir. I'll have a look."

"Hurry it up, man! Everything's planned to time."

The chauffeur descended into the dark lane and then turned the spotlight on the car's side towards the bonnet. With the bonnet raised he tinkered for a while with the engine, and at last scratched the back of his neck.

"Well?" Gordon demanded anxiously.

"Afraid there's nothing I can do here, sir. The ignition's at fault and I can't see to repair it. I'll have to phone for a patrol-man or a garage."

Gordon tugged out his pocket watch. It was 6:30.

"There won't be a garage until you reach Ascot," he said, "and that's three miles away. The Little Ashton railway station is over to the left there. I'd better head for it and get a local to London. You fix the car up."

"Right, sir! But I thought you said you weren't taking a train no matter what happened?"

"I've got to in this case, otherwise I'll miss that meeting. The car business may be a long job. Get my suitcase from the back, will you?"

The chauffeur obeyed and in a moment, started out of his complacency by the sudden turn in events, Gordon was heading across a deserted field in the direction of the dreary lights that marked the station, or rather a wayside halt. He had practically reached it, was passing the crumbled brickwork of an ancient railway bridge where the track had once been laid, when he fancied he caught the sound of footsteps behind him. Puzzled, he stopped, peering into the murk. The light just where he was standing was fairly clear, coming from the station lamps, but once beyond their range there was only the dark.

He wondered for a moment if perhaps the chauffeur was following him up, then all his speculations were dashed as he was abruptly seized from behind. His traveling case fell out of his grasp and he was fighting for his life with every ounce of the vast strength Tensile-X could give him, and the strength was there: no doubt of that. As yet its power did not seem in the least diminished. With one terrific blow he felled his attacker to the ground, then peered at him narrowly as he struggled up again.

"Blessington!" Gordon exclaimed, recognizing the worn, tired face, and haunted eyes.

"Yes, Blessington! I've been waiting a long time for this, Mr. Cocksure Fryer! Ever since the night when you told me to get out of the Larches! I've tried everything and you've always been one jump ahead of me, but since I came out of jail I made up my mind to keep constant track of you, personally, and hope for just one moment like this."

"So it was you who fixed my car!"

"'Course it was! I kept watch on your house. I knew where you were heading, because the papers have been full of it, and I guessed correctly that you'd go alone except for the chauffeur. I got on to the rear bumper, pretty wide on that limousine of yours. To stop the car all I had to do was stuff my handkerchief in the exhaust pipe at the appropriate moment, which was easy enough by leaning over the bumper. Your chauffeur never thought of such a gag, having no particular reason to. I thought you'd be left alone in the car while he went for help, but this is just as good. I came on ahead of you and I'm going to finish you!"

Gordon waited tensely, not so much because he was afraid of his sworn enemy but because he could see the penultimate photograph of the Scanner coming true. The crumbled walls of the ruined bridge and the lights from the station to the rear. Even his clothes. His hat, though in the photograph it had looked like a homburg, was actually not one. But there was no gainsaying, now he came to swiftly reflect, that it was identical in silhouette to the one in the photograph.

Next there should be a knife. He ought to struggle with his enemy, and he did. Almost before he realized it. With a sudden overflow of vengeful anger Blessington hurled himself forward, a knife in his grasp.

"If I'd been able to get a gun you wouldn't be alive now, curse you!" he panted, and with that he slashed the blade downwards. It ripped the front of Gordon's coat, and in normal circumstances it would also have inflicted a deep gash down his chest. As it was his tremendous resistance saved him.

It was plain that Blessington was astounded that his attack had no effect, and the next moment he was in no position to consider the matter. Gordon whipped the knife from his grasp and drove it downwards, again and again, hardly realizing what he was doing in his furious determination to be rid of his enemy.

Blessington groaned and choked, then slid down into the stubbly grass. Gordon peered at him and the knife dropped from his fingers. In a few seconds he had discovered that Blessington was dead, stabbed through the heart.

Panting, Gordon looked about him. His overcoat was slashed and bloodstained from the attack; the leg of his tweed trousers was ripped away from the knee where he had caught it on a tree stump. To go to the station in this condition would simply be asking for an enquiry.

He did the only possible thing. Quickly he tore off his overcoat and then his suit, replacing it with the dress suit he had in his traveling case and fitting a bow tie to his white collar where he had been wearing a long green tie. His torn suit he pushed in the case and then hurried to the fallen remains of the bridge and hid it amongst the brickwork.

He next grabbed Blessington's body and dragged it to the spot near the hidden suitcase, rearranging fallen bricks to conceal the corpse as much as possible.

This done Gordon looked about him, breathing hard. All was quiet. Then the sound of a distant train approaching the station halt startled him. He adjusted his hat, threw his blood-stained overcoat over his arm, so that the lining was outwards and hurried to the station as fast as he could go. He arrived just as the train was approaching.

"This train go to London?" he demanded of the station master-cum-porter.

"It does. Single or return?" The old man's eye registered a faint astonishment at the sight of the prosperous, fleshy individual in the dress suit, with his face dirty and worried. It didn't make sense.

"Single—and hurry!" Gordon paid, grabbed his ticket, then tumbled into the train with seconds to spare. To his relief he found he'd hit upon an empty compartment. Slowly he relaxed, weighing up the situation. He was grimly conscious of the fact that the trend of events had forced him into a dress suit after all, and in sudden alarm, he looked at the window of the train, then sighed in relief. There was no trace of a bill in reverse saying 'Rugby', as there had been on the last-act photograph. Nor was he wearing a wristwatch. For that matter, his hat and overcoat did not tally with those in the photograph, either.

"Which makes me safe," he muttered. "Once that confounded banquet's over, I'll ditch the dress suit and get another suit from somewhere. I've been stampeded so far, but this is where it stops. As for Blessington—" His mouth tightened as he already weighed up how he would plead self defense if anything were ever traced to him.

Probably his satisfaction would not have been so complete had he been able to view the station-halt he had just left. Through the rickety gateway that led to the platform two men in raincoats and bowler hats stepped actively, finally nailing the stationmaster in his ticket booth.

"Seen a man around here, early middle age, city type, wearing a dark trilby hat and a brown overcoat?"

It was the taller of the two men who fired the questions, and the stationmaster was not such a rustic that he could not detect two plainclothes detectives.

"Come to think of it, yes. He'd got a dirty face, evening dress, and a coat over his arm."

"Where'd he go? Take a train to London?"

"That's right. Single."

"When's the next train from this cockeyed hole?"

"Be another hour."

"All right, never mind. Thanks."

The tall man jerked his head and his companion followed him back across the field from the station.

"We can reach London quicker in the car," the tall man said. "Bit of a queer business this. We're told to act as bodyguard to Fryer and never let him get far out of our sight, and now we find murder. No guarantee he did it, but it looks mighty like it, especially since that's the body of Blessington."

"And Fryer's suit in the case," the shorter man added.

"Uh-huh! We'd better hurry."

The situation here existing was simply explained. Detailed by Chief Inspector Bland to keep a watch on the welfare of Gordon Fryer, the two men had followed his car at a respectable distance when it had started on its journey, they knowing even as Blessington had, that his destination was London to attend the Inventors' Convention. They had caught up with the limousine to find it empty and broken down. Their investigation of the car had hardly finished before the return of the chauffeur from the road telephone. To discover where Gordon had gone had not taken long, but the finding of a knife in the stubble grass, which the taller man had accidentally kicked, had led the two law hounds automatically to the discovery of the dead Blessington and the abandoned suitcase. So now they were no longer the protectors but the hunters. Everything pointed to Gordon Fryer being a murderer, and no matter what plea he might make he had got to be arrested.

Meanwhile Gordon was cursing the slowness of the train as it stopped at every station *en route*. Ascot—

Egham—Staines. Then at last to Hounslow, Brentford, and the environs of London. It seemed he would never get to the capital, but he made it finally and plunged into a taxi, more thankful than he could say that he was out of the train without mishap. On the return journey he would use a taxi: of this he was determined.

It was five to eight when he reached the great edifice designated to the Incorporated Society of Inventors, which gave him five minutes to wash, brush up, and generally effect an air of goodwill. When he arrived in the midst of the assembly he looked quite undisturbed, even though, inwardly, his feelings were chaotic.

The dinner itself seemed to take an interminable time and he would much have preferred to decline food, but manners had to be observed. Even longer seemed the speeches afterwards. Now and again he glanced at his watch, remembering that the fatal moment, according to the wristwatch in the photograph, was 11:03. On the last occasion at which he consulted his watch the time was 9:40, but it was at least a quarter to eleven before he himself was called to ascend the rostrum.

Smiling benevolently, he did as he was asked, and the chairman of the Society held up his hand to quell the conversation in the great hall.

"Ladies and gentlemen, as all of you are aware, we are assembled here tonight not only because it is our annual convention dinner, but to do honor to the greatest inventor of the present day. No single inventor has brought two such great benefits to Mankind as Spiritine and the Fryer Eye. The latter invention in particular ranks in importance with the discoveries of Rontgen, Lister, Madame Curie, and others—"

"Hear, hear!"

"We feel—" the Chairman continued, pouring forth eulogy, and Gordon's eyes strayed from him to the intent faces of the assembly, and then beyond them to the great doors at the rear of the hall. He gave a start as he beheld two men who had the unmistakable stamp of detectives about them, and a policeman in uniform was a little way beyond them.

"—to say a few words," the Chairman finished, and with an effort Gordon jerked himself back to reality.

"Just a few words," Mr. Fryer, before I make the presentation on behalf of us all," the Chairman smiled.

"Presentation? Er—yes, of course." Gordon pulled his gaze from the three waiting figures at the back of the hall. Blessington! They must have found the body somehow! They were waiting to make an arrest! There could not be any other reason for two detectives and a constable. In his panic he had forgotten that he had asked for police protection.

The Chairman moved uneasily. Gordon realized this, mopped his forehead, then spoke:

"Mr. Chairman, ladies and gentlemen, I must ask you to forgive my apparent nervousness tonight, but, well, this is rather an alarming ovation. If I had my own way I'd much sooner have stayed at home!"

There was good-natured laughter and no comprehension of the fact that Gordon spoke from the heart.

"What more can I say than thank you exceedingly

for your kindness and appreciation of my inventive capacity? If I have helped civilization and humanity on its way by my efforts, then I am more than repaid."

There would have been no point in him speaking further in any case for the applause was deafening. When it subsided, he found the Chairman before him again, this time holding an oblong box in his palm.

"Mr. Fryer," he said quietly, "I deliberately omitted to mention your famous 'Forever Watch'. Your connection with it in company with Dr. Royd, is well known, and the public in general have much to thank you for. We considered it fitting, although I observe you use an old-fashioned dress watch, that our presentation to you should be one of your own famous watches, not the pattern that everybody in the world uses, but an exclusive one, which we, the Society of Inventors, have devised. It is of solid gold and inscribed by us, to you."

Gordon stared dumbly as the box opened. On the plush bed within lay the very watch that he believed he would never encounter. It was the one in the photograph! The—

"I don't want it," he said abruptly. "Where would be the sense of two watches? I have one, and a good one. I—"

"Oh, come now, Mr. Fryer!" the Chairman laughed. "We shall feel terribly offended if you refuse our offering. In fact you shan't!" he broke off resolutely, and before Gordon grasped what was happening his left wrist had been seized and the watch bracelet clamped about it. It clicked, and he knew better than anybody living that only a file could remove it.

"There!" the Chairman smiled. "Not so terrible, is it?"

Gordon said nothing, his eyes flaming with angry fear, the audience clapping thunderously.

The Chairman looked puzzled, quite unable to understand such aversion to such a costly gift, then suddenly Gordon saw again the three implacable figures at the back of the hall.

He could control himself no longer. Wheeling, he plunged for the doorway at the rear of the rostrum and dived through it, leaving an astounded assembly wondering what had happened.

The moment he was in the passage beyond the hall Gordon hurtled to the cloakroom, looking over his shoulder as he did so. Still expecting pursuit, he felt for his hat and coat, grabbed them, and departed at top speed. He said no word to the surprised doorkeeper, his whole concentration being on escaping as fast as possible into the night.

Down the alley he ran, scrambling into his hat and coat as he went. Reaching the main street he signaled a taxi but it went sailing by, evidently bent on some other errand. Nor, at the moment, did there appear to be any others in sight.

Muttering to himself, Gordon raced along the pavement, giving a look back ever and again, and presently, to his alarm, he saw a police patrol car speeding in his direction. Immediately he ducked down a side road and raced up an incline, to find himself abruptly in a great wide space filled with the din of trains and rattle of milk cans. He realized that unexpectedly he had entered a railway station, but which it was—King's Cross, Euston, or St. Pancras—he had no idea.

He dragged to a standstill, filled with deadening horror as he perceived how completely he had sidetracked himself into coming again within the radius of trains. Immediately he turned about, to retreat the way he had come, but the distant vision of hurrying men deterred him. He gave a desperate glance around and then plunged into the midst of the people milling about the great space. In so doing he looked up at the clock and nearly wept with relief.

It was 11:15! Twelve minutes after the fatal time shown on the Scanner photograph. The sight of the clock so fascinated him he remained staring at it for a moment, making sure it had not stopped! No, the hand was moving, all right.

"Eleven-fifteen," he whispered. "Thank God! The Scanner was wrong! I've proved it!"

He was so deliriously pleased with himself he wanted to tell everybody; then he came back to the difficult situation. He had managed transiently to lose himself in the crowd. That meant that all exits from the station would probably be watched. The only other way out was a train, whether he liked it or not.

"Not that it can matter," he whispered to himself. "It can't matter, you fool! The time's gone past now. It's twenty past eleven and the photograph said three minutes past! And you're still alive! The Scanner's wrong!"

He stopped muttering, facing the indicator board. He ran his eye down the train departure list. There was a train for Reading at 11:25. He nodded to himself and moved away—then he remembered he hadn't looked from which platform the train was due to depart.

With an effort he could just see the number as a man in front of the indicator board moved slightly. Platform 2. If Gordon had waited two seconds longer for his unknown fellow traveler to completely move aside he would have seen that the number was actually 12, the '1' being hidden for the moment by the man's body.

But Gordon did not know, and the relentless threads woven in his destiny were tightening all around him. He bought his ticket and then raced for Platform 2. The train was in, but to his surprise no inspector was at the barrier. He went through, settled in the train, and closed his eyes whilst he recovered his shattered nerves.

Presently the delay in starting occurred to him and he looked out of the open window. It was 11:30 now, but the train was just getting on the move.

"Five minutes late," he muttered. "Why in hell railways can't stick to time I don't know."

He settled down again breathing hard, watching the lights of the station flashing by. Then over the points and the train was well on its journey. Gordon looked about him, somewhat puzzled. This compartment was a corridor, a most unusual thing for a local train to Reading. But at least it explained why there had been no inspector at the barrier: tickets could be collected on the train. But as the train was not long-distance, it did not make sense.

"What the—" Gordon began, the grip of fear at his heart again; then he gave a violent start as, for the first time in his hectic flight, he noticed his overcoat. It was not his own! It fitted reasonably well, but it definitely was not his property. It was a subdued check pattern with raglan shoulders. Startled, he pulled off his hat. That too fitted well, but again it did not belong to him. He sat staring at it, too frozen with horror to think straight. Then, by degrees, like drops of icy water, the answers to his questions came to him.

In dashing into the cloakroom he had looked behind him, and again when he had snatched down his hat and coat. He must have accidentally whipped down the hat and coat next to his own, and in his frantic excitement he had not even bothered to notice what he was wearing.

"The photograph!" he panted, sweating. "These were in the photograph! Same hat, same coat—" His burning eyes looked towards the window. There was no label saying 'Rugby'. He relaxed a little, returned the hat to his head, then mopped his face.

"It can't happen!" he told himself passionately. "It can't! It's gone past the time! The Scanner's a liar— Hey!" he broke off sharply as an inspector went along the corridor.

"Yes, sir?" The inspector came in, unable to hide his surprise at the distraught look on Gordon's face.

"Where am I?" Gordon demanded. "What train is this?"

"The eleven-thirty to Crewe, sir."

"What!" Gordon jumped up. "It can't be! It's the eleven twenty-five for Reading!"

"Sorry, sir. You've made a mistake somewhere. Crewe first stop, with connections for the North and Scotland—"

"I haven't made a mistake!" Gordon shouted. "Platform 2 for the Reading train! I saw it distinctly on the indicator board."

"Twelve, sir," the guard insisted. "That's the one which goes out as far at Watford and then turns back to go south to Reading. Normally, the Reading trains go from Victoria."

"Then where in hell did this one start from?"

The guard looked astonished. "Euston, sir—naturally."

"Euston—Euston," Gordon muttered to himself. "Yes, I suppose it must have been, nearest station to the Society."

"Anything more, sir?" the guard asked laconically.

"No. No thanks."

"I'll check with you later, sir, about the extra amount for your ticket."

"A moment! You say this is a through train?"

"Yes, sir. Crewe first stop."

Gordon nodded, staring fixedly before him. The guard half turned to go and then hesitated.

"You're Mr. Gordon Fryer, sir, aren't you?" he asked.

"I recognize you now."

"Yes. I'm Gordon Fryer."

Respect came into the inspector's voice. "Anything wrong, Mr. Fryer? Not feeling very well?"

"Just leave me alone," Gordon muttered. "And keep your eyes open for an accident. There may be one to this train."

"Oh?" the guard looked unconvinced, which was not very surprising.

"I'm not sure, just maybe," Gordon said. "Depends on the time factor. Something's wrong somewhere. Oh, get out!" he shouted suddenly, so the guard went, frowning to himself.

Gordon sat down again slowly, looking at the blank seat opposite him. "Eleven-three was the time," he whispered. "Now it's—" He felt for his pocket watch and then stopped, conscious of the presentation watch on his wrist. So comfortably did it fit he had forgotten all about it. From the way he looked at it, it might have been the head of a striking snake.

It said exactly 11:03!

Mechanically he raised it to his ear to catch the faint sound of the internal transformer; but the watch was utterly dead. The sweep hand was not moving. Again the answer slowly came to him. It must have been put on his wrist at exactly that time, but his bodily condition, governed as it had been and still was, by extreme fear, had prevented the watch from operating. Nobody knew better than he how quickly a fault in the rhythm of the body could stop the watch functioning.

11:03! Slowly he realized he had had no other clue as to the time of his death except the watch. As long as it stayed at 11:03, he could die any time and still keep faith with the damnable last-act photograph!

Suddenly hysterical terror seized him and he pulled savagely at the bracelet, but so well was it made, after his own original design, he could not budge it. Finally he stopped, panting, wondering whether he should ask the guard for a nail file or something. Somehow, he did not feel up to making the effort. There was a curious sensation inside him, a feeling of deadly weariness as though his bones had turned to jelly. He had never felt like this in his life before. With Tensile-X having built him up into a man of iron, he surely ought not to have symptoms like these?

Yet he had. He just could not rise to his feet but sat there stunned, wondering at the queer flabbiness coming over him.

Footsteps in the corridor roused him and to his surprise the guard returned, a long oblong slip of paper in his hand. From the look of it the slip was wet.

"Sorry to bother you, sir," he apologized. "Must just stick this on the window here. This section of train has to be taken back to Rugby from Crewe. Means you'll have to change too, sir."

With an effort Gordon turned his head. Deftly the guard slapped the label in reverse on to the top of the window glass; then he left the compartment.

Gordon could not take his eyes from that label. His powers of reasoning were not functioning properly any more. Something was wrong. His bones felt like water. He could hardly sit up straight....

The carriage swung as points rattled and clicked under the wheels, and the force of the swing threw Gordon on his side, his left arm dangling. For all his efforts he could not get up again.

He was abruptly startled by the sound of another oncoming train hurtling past the windows. From the other side flashed and flickered the lights of a station, filling the compartment with a brief, bewildering glare.

Gordon knew then that he had reached the end of the road. There was to be no collision. The light had come from the station and an oncoming train flashing past. He half-smiled to himself, glad to relax into the drowning tide of darkness.

His dangling arm swung back and forth with the train's incessant motion, and the noise of the rail-joints seemed to constantly be repeating eleven-three... eleven-three...eleven-three...eleven-three....

ABOUT THE AUTHOR

British writer JOHN RUSSELL FEARN was born near Manchester, England, in 1908. As a child he devoured the science fiction of Wells and Verne, and was a voracious reader of the Boys' Story Papers. He was also fascinated by the cinema, and first broke into print in 1931 with a series of articles in *Film Weekly.*

He then quickly sold his first novel, *The Intelligence Gigantic*, to the American magazine, *Amazing Stories.* Over the next fifteen years, writing under several pseudonyms, Fearn became one of the most prolific contributors to all of the leading US science fiction pulps, including such legendary publications as *Astounding Stories, Startling Stories, Thrilling Wonder Stories,* and *Weird Tales.*

During the late 1940s he diversified into writing novels for the UK market, and also created his famous superwoman character, The Golden Amazon, for the prestigious Canadian magazine, the Toronto *Star Weekly.* In the early 1950s in the UK, his fifty-two novels as "Vargo Statten" were bestsellers, most notably his novelization of the film, *Creature from the Black Lagoon.*

Apart from science fiction, he had equal success with westerns, romances, and detective fiction, writing an amazing total of 180 novels—most of them in a period of just ten years—before his early death in 1960. His work has been translated into nine languages, and continues to be reprinted and read worldwide.

www.ingramcontent.com/pod-product-compliance
Lightning Source LLC
Chambersburg PA
CBHW031429250626
47155CB00004B/1672